"Told you Sam would show," Matthew said.

Mr. Vaughn reached into his pocket and tossed a coin to Matthew, who caught it.

Matthew winked at her. "He bet me two bits you wouldn't come."

Samantha didn't know why his wink had made her feel as though they shared an intimate secret or why she found the slight curve of his lip intriguing. He wasn't looking at her the way that a boy looked at a girl in whom he had an interest. But she suddenly realized that she might be staring at him as a girl would . . . because it dawned on her with unexpected clarity that Matthew Hart was as handsome as sin.

AN AVON TRUE ROMANCE

Samantha
and the
Cowboy

LORRAINE HEATH

AVON BOOKS
An Imprint of HarperCollinsPublishers

FIND TRUE LOVE!
www.avontrueromance.com

An Avon True Romance is a trademark of HarperCollins Publishers, Inc.

Samantha and the Cowboy

Copyright © 2002 by Jan Nowasky

Printed in the United States of America.
For information address HarperCollins Children's Books,
a division of HarperCollins Publishers, 1350 Avenue of the Americas,
New York, NY 10019.

Library of Congress Catalog Card Number: 2001118668
ISBN 0-06-447341-4

First Avon edition, 2002

AVON TRADEMARK REG. U.S. PAT. OFF. AND IN OTHER COUNTRIES,
MARCA REGISTRADA, HECHO EN U.S.A.

Visit us on the World Wide Web!
www.harperteen.com

For Brandon and Alex

May your journeys lead you toward your dreams

and the roads you travel always guide you home

CHAPTER ONE

Faithful, Texas
1866

WANTED!
BOYS FOURTEEN AND OLDER TO HERD CATTLE
TO SEDALIA, MISSOURI.
WILL BE PAID $100 AT END OF DRIVE.
IF INTERESTED, SEE THE TRAIL BOSS AT 7 IN
THE MORNING OUTSIDE THE GENERAL STORE.

With her heart thundering, Samantha Reynolds read the notice that someone had tacked to the wall outside the general store. A hundred dollars seemed like a fortune. What she wouldn't give to be a boy, so she could have the opportunity to earn that money for her family!

At sixteen she could barely remember the last time that coins had jingled in her reticule. Mr. Thomas, the owner of the general store, allowed her family to buy on credit. He kept a tally of supplies purchased and debts owed. Samantha didn't want to consider how long their tally sheet was getting to be. It had been months since her mother had been able to hand any money over to Mr. Thomas.

At this very moment her older brother, Benjamin, was loading their most recent purchases into the wagon. At twenty, he was old enough to be hired for the cattle drive. But she knew it would be nearly impossible to convince him to go. Since he'd returned from the war that had devastated many of the southern states, he was reluctant to do anything that took him away from their farm.

Her sister Amy was fourteen, old enough. But just like Samantha, she wasn't a boy. Her younger brother, Nate, was only twelve. He wouldn't qualify.

Samantha thought about the bolt of blue calico she'd seen inside the store. She wanted to sew a new dress, but the material was expensive as all get-out at ten cents a yard. She was wasting her time longing for it and hankering for any of the frippery and finery that the general store was slowly starting to stock, now that the war had ended.

Still, she did yearn for things. She wanted the life she'd had before the War against Northern Aggression, as most folks in these parts referred to it. She longed for people to start laughing again. Or if they couldn't laugh, at least to smile once in a while.

A hundred dollars wouldn't return life to the way it had been, but it would purchase several bolts of calico, canned goods to last through the winter, a new hoe, some chickens, a cow, and too many other things to count. She got dizzy with the possibilities swirling through her mind.

"I think we ought to have us a spring dance," the girl standing beside her on the boardwalk said.

Lost in thought, Samantha had almost forgotten Mary Margaret Anderson had been visiting with her. They'd been best friends forever. They'd sat beside each other in the one-room schoolhouse until they were fourteen and passed the exam that proclaimed they knew all that was to be taught. They'd shared confidences and dreams.

"We finally have some fiddle players in the area, and most of the boys learned to play a harmonica while they were away," Mary Margaret added.

"Do you even know how to dance?" Samantha asked distractedly, more interested in the notice than in dancing. If she stared at it long enough, maybe the words would change to include girls.

"For pity's sake, Samantha Jane, I could learn," Mary Margaret told her. "So could you."

"Why would I want to learn to dance?"

"Because we're growing up!" Mary Margaret pointed out.

Samantha knew she should be excited at the possibility of attending a dance, but she had very little interest in boys. She remembered a time when she'd raced against them, climbed trees with them, even on a few occasions wrestled with them, but that was years ago.

Before most of the boys in the area had run off to join the army as soon as they were old enough to beat a drum.

She'd matured into a young woman with no males around to speak of, except for those who were too old to fight and those too young to hold a weapon. She'd experienced no dances or Sunday picnics or peering coyly beneath her eyelashes at a young man across the classroom. The war had taken the young men from the classroom and placed them on the battlefields.

Although many had returned home, none had struck her fancy. Mary Margaret was constantly talking about boys. How handsome Jeremy was, or what pretty eyes Luke had.

If Samantha noticed boys at all, she noticed how strong they looked, mentally figuring how many acres of land they could plow in a day. She certainly had no desire to have one stepping on her toes while they danced.

She didn't want to talk about the local boys or the possibility of a dance. She preferred to discuss ways to ease her mother's burden, but once Mary Margaret turned her mind to a subject, she stuck with it.

"Do you think Benjamin would ask me to dance?" Mary Margaret asked.

Samantha snapped her gaze to Mary Margaret. She had her complete attention now. "Benjamin?"

She was surprised to see twin spots of red appear on Mary Margaret's cheeks.

"I think your brother is fine looking," Mary Margaret admitted.

"Do you fancy him?" Samantha asked. She'd never thought of her brother attracting any girl's attention—least of all Mary Margaret's.

"Of course I do. Not that it does me any good. I'm invisible, as far as he's concerned." Frustration rippled through her voice.

"Benjamin isn't noticing much of anything these days," Samantha said kindly. Benjamin had returned from the war minus an arm. She didn't blame him for resenting his loss, but it did seem that his anger was hurting him more than anything else had. "He's still adjusting to coming home not quite whole."

"Lots of fellas lost limbs," Mary Margaret said. "Benjamin is still strong, though."

"He needs something to help him get his confidence back," Samantha mused. She touched the notice. "I wish I could get him to consider doing this."

Mary Margaret glanced at the notice. "How long does it take to get cattle from here to Sedalia?"

"A couple of months, I suspect," Samantha said quietly.

"Then I hope he won't do it. It would only take him away from me for a spell, and he was gone long enough."

"But a hundred dollars." Samantha sighed wistfully. "We could do a lot with that money. I'd go if I could."

Mary Margaret's eyes widened. "It's calling for boys. Not girls."

"Which isn't fair," Samantha told her. "I'm just as capable as any fella."

"Samantha Jane!" Benjamin called out. "Wagon's loaded. Let's go."

Samantha tore her gaze away from the notice. "Benjamin, did you see this?"

Wearing his usual scowl, her older brother ambled over.

"Hello, Benjamin," Mary Margaret said coyly.

Samantha had never seen her friend bat her eyelashes so rapidly.

"You got something in your eye?" Benjamin asked.

Mary Margaret stilled her eyelashes. "No."

Samantha felt a pang for her friend. Why couldn't Benjamin notice Mary Margaret the way she wanted to be noticed? She wondered if she'd have as much trouble getting a young man's attention if she ever found one who piqued her interest.

Pouting, Mary Margaret said, "Guess I'll see if my pa's ready to go."

Mary Margaret disappeared into the general store.

"You could have been nicer to her, Benjamin," Samantha scolded.

"I showed concern about her eyes. If she didn't have something in them, what was her problem? Did she develop a nervous twitch during the war?"

She didn't know whether to laugh or feel sorry for him. She definitely pitied Mary Margaret for setting her sights on Benjamin. "She was flirting."

He furrowed his brow. "Flirtin'? With me?"

"Do you see any other man standing around here?"

"Why would she flirt with me?"

"Because she hasn't got a lick of sense," Samantha said under her breath. She tapped the notice on the wall, drawing his attention back to the reason she'd called him over. "Did you see this?"

She waited impatiently while he read the notice, then she blurted, "You could do that, Benjamin—join that outfit, go on that cattle drive."

"They need men with two arms," he grumbled as he turned away. "Let's go."

Disappointment reeling through her, she took one last longing look at the notice. Why couldn't she have been born a boy?

"Samantha Jane!" Benjamin hollered. "Stop dawdling!"

She scurried to the wagon and clambered onto the

bench seat beside her brother. Slipping her bonnet over her head, she jerked the ribbons into a bow beneath her chin. Why wouldn't he even consider the possibility that he *could* do it? If only she wasn't a girl, she'd sign up in a heartbeat. Heck fire, she'd already be waiting in line.

With a quick flick of his wrist, Benjamin set the horses and the wagon into motion.

She'd been terrified that Benjamin wouldn't return from the war . . . and in a way, he hadn't. The reticent young man sitting beside her now baffled her. He didn't seem to care about anyone or anything. He'd been badly wounded at Shiloh. He'd lost his arm during the battle he wouldn't even talk about. But he was still healthy and strong. And working on a cattle drive would bring in a lot more money than the crops.

She glanced over her shoulder at the pitifully small amount of supplies that Mr. Thomas had allowed them to purchase on credit today. Flour. Sugar. Nothing beyond the essentials. She didn't consider herself greedy, but it was difficult when all their hard work never gave them enough for something extra. And what would they do when Mr. Thomas got tired of doling out credit?

"I thought cowboys just rode their horses and kept the cattle plodding in a straight line," she said quietly as they passed by the bank. It was the only brick building in town.

"Usually. Unless there's a stampede, or a flood, or cattle rustlers. A man's gotta have two good arms. That's all there is to it," he said.

"Couldn't you at least give it a try?" she asked.

"Nope."

She thought about the worry lines in her mother's face. Lines that had deepened since her pa had gotten sick and died of pneumonia three years before. Why did life have to be so hard?

Why couldn't she have been born a boy?

Later that night Samantha lay in bed beside her younger sister. Amy had fallen asleep shortly after Samantha had blown out the flame on the candle. But sleep wasn't coming as easily to Samantha.

Staring through her window at the stars glittering in the midnight sky, she was hoping to catch sight of one as it fell so she could make a wish. A wish for better times.

A wish that her mother wouldn't look so tired. That the dark circles beneath her eyes would fade. That the furrows in her brow caused by worry wouldn't run so deeply.

That Benjamin wouldn't be so unhappy. That he'd realize he was alive, and that reason alone was cause to rejoice. That he might come to understand why Mary

Margaret wanted his attention.

For all her wishes, she needed more than one falling star. She wished that Amy could have a new dress instead of always having to wear Samantha's worn and frayed hand-me-downs.

She wished that her younger brother, Nate, wouldn't have to leave the table hungry. At twelve, he was heading into his growing years. Ma kept saying he must have a hollow leg because he ate so much but stayed hungry. Samantha had noticed how her mother wasn't eating very much of late. She'd started giving most of her helping to Nate. Samantha had begun to do the same thing.

Right now, crops were plentiful, but what would they do come winter? Would they have enough to see them through?

She just couldn't stop thinking about that promise of a hundred dollars. If only Nate was a little older, he'd probably go on that cattle drive. She wondered if Ma would lie about his age so he could go. A lie seemed like such a small thing when Samantha thought of all they would gain. Nate would leave here with empty pockets and come back with coins a-jingling. Was a white lie really that Gawd-awful?

They'd be able to pay off their debt to the general store. They could stock up on cans of food and dry staples for the winter. Maybe they could even purchase a new milk cow. Old Bess was truly getting old.

But Samantha couldn't see her mother telling a lie—or letting Nate go off on his own. He was her baby, after all.

Samantha sighed wistfully. *I'm old enough and not afraid of hard work. If only I were a boy.*

If only . . .

Her heart started to pound, sending the blood thrumming between her temples. She was old enough. She wouldn't have to lie about her age. She wouldn't even have to fib about her name if she were to shorten it. Hadn't her pa always called her Sam when she'd worked in the fields with him?

Glancing at her sleeping sister, she eased out of bed. The moonlight streaming through the window guided her to the dresser. Carefully she struck a match and lit the tallow candle. The tiny flame quivered as though it dreaded her thoughts. She looked over her shoulder at Amy to make certain she hadn't disturbed her. She still slept soundly.

Samantha moved the candle closer to the mirror as she gazed at her reflection. She wouldn't call her features delicate. Not like Mary Margaret's. However, she wouldn't classify herself as plain, either. Just not overly fragile looking.

Samantha knew the only things about her person

that truly identified her as female were her long reddish hair and the gentle swells on her chest. Scissors could get rid of the long strands, and binding would eliminate the evidence of her breasts. She could flatten them with a long length of material, something from her mother's quilting basket, wound tightly around her chest. A little dirt on her cheeks and chin to hide the fact that she had no whiskers . . .

She ran her hand down her face. She'd miss her hair. Her mother called it her crowning glory. But it would grow back. Eventually.

A hundred dollars. Just for guiding a few cattle north. How hard could that particular task be?

She considered tucking her hair up under her hat, but if a good strong wind sent the hat sailing over the prairie, her secret would be revealed. She couldn't risk letting that happen. No one wanted a woman on a cattle drive.

And yet she knew she was as capable as any boy. After Benjamin had left for the war, Samantha had stepped into his boots, taking on the role of the eldest. Doing what had to be done without being asked. Plowing the fields, harvesting the crops, mending fences, caring for sick livestock. She'd even had to put down an animal or two.

Then when her pa had died, she'd become the one

person whom her mother leaned on. Samantha was accustomed to being independent, making decisions. She didn't ask her mother what chores needed doing. She simply did them.

Heck fire! She wanted to earn that hundred dollars with a desperation that was almost frightening. It would help ease some of her mother's burdens. She wasn't naïve enough to think it would solve all their problems. But it would go a powerful long way toward lightening the load.

She set the candle on the dresser. The quivering light cast an eerie faint halo around her. Slowly she unraveled her long braid. When she was finished, her hair cascaded around her like a heavy curtain. She combed her fingers through the thick tresses that reached below her waist. Her crowning glory. It would grow back in time.

She knelt in front of her sewing basket and lifted the lid. She removed the scissors. They were cold against her fingers.

She gathered her courage around her like a warm blanket in winter. *We need the money. Desperately.*

Unfolding her body, she took one last glance at her reflection in the mirror. Using only her thumb and forefinger, she took hold of several strands of hair and lifted them straight up. Her heart thundered so loudly that she imagined it sounded like the hooves of cattle pounding the earth during a stampede.

It's only hair, she thought. Closing her eyes and shuddering, she took the first snip.

She felt the fallen tresses float against her nightgown before they landed on the floor with an ominous silence. Opening her eyes, she cringed at the sight of the shortened strands curling just above her brow.

It wasn't too late to turn back. To crawl into bed and forget this hare-brained idea of hers. To leave the remainder of her hair alone.

But in a way, she knew it had been too late the moment she had read the notice that had been posted outside the general store. She'd offered Benjamin the chance to help out the family, and he'd turned her down flat.

Nothing got done if a person thought it couldn't be done. Samantha knew she could do this.

Grabbing more strands of hair, she released a quaking breath and went to work. Cut and snip, cut and snip, cut and snip. Her stomach tightened with each bite of the scissors.

Within the mirror, the contours of her face seemed to change. The soft lines faded as though they mourned the loss of her hair. Her eyes seemed to grow larger, her cheekbones harsher.

When she lopped off the final strands, she sank onto a nearby chair, her knees wobbly and unable to support her. With tears welling in her eyes, she stared at the reflection in the mirror.

What had she done?

Samantha had disappeared. And in her place staring out of the mirror was Sam.

CHAPTER TWO

Samantha—Sam, she had to remember her name was now Sam—stood outside the general store, her knees quaking. Her stomach felt as though someone had tied a noosed rope around it and was tugging hard.

Two men stood in front of her. Men, not boys. A few men and boys stood behind her.

It seemed several people were as desperate as she was to earn a hundred dollars. Fortunately, she didn't know any of these fellas. Since the war, so many men were drifting aimlessly from place to place, never stopping long enough to put down roots. Those she did know were farmers who couldn't risk leaving their fields.

She knew she was taking a chance that the crops would suffer without her to care for them. But her mother had Nate and Amy. And even though Benjamin grumbled that he was useless, he did what he could, and she thought he did a fine job of working the fields.

In the cold shadows, long before dawn, she'd sneaked through the house to Nate's room and grabbed a pair of his britches, a flannel shirt, and an old coat. Nate was just a little bigger than she was, even though he was four years younger. She'd located a battered black hat that had belonged to her pa. It made her feel closer to him, to think he might approve of her scheme.

Leaving her mother a note explaining that she needed to go to town, she'd saddled her brown mare, Cinnamon, and headed on in. A thousand times during the journey, she'd questioned her sanity. A hundred times she'd almost turned around. But her family's needs were greater than her fears.

Her desire to help her family greatly outweighed her terror of the unknown, of the dangers that might lie ahead.

Benjamin may have let the war defeat him, but she wasn't going to allow it to get the best of her.

Her mouth grew dry as the first man in line moved aside and the next fella stepped up to give his particulars to a man sitting behind a small table. She'd heard it whispered about that he was the trail boss. The one she had to impress. The one who could crush her dreams with a single word—or give them flight.

Suddenly the hairs on the nape of her neck began to prickle. Unease settled around her. Slowly she let her gaze wander . . . and then it slammed to a stop.

A young man was leaning against the side of the building, a short distance away from the table. Why hadn't she noticed him earlier? Had he been there all along? Was he hoping to get hired on with this outfit? If so, why wasn't he standing in line? Maybe he'd been hired before she'd arrived, and he was saving a place for the other hired men to wait.

He had his arms folded across his chest, his hat brim pulled down low so she couldn't get a good look at his eyes, but she knew those eyes were trained on her. She could feel his gaze boring into her, was acutely aware of him studying her. He had a hardness about him, as though he hoped to find fault with her. Was her disguise not as good as she'd thought it was?

"Next."

Her breath started coming in shallow little pants as though it was as afraid as she was that the fella would figure out she was a girl. She brushed away the thought just as she'd brushed dirt on her cheeks and chin earlier. She was worrying for nothing. For pity's sake, he probably wasn't even looking at her. He stood so still that he might have been a statue . . . or asleep. He was probably—

"Next!"

She jerked to attention. The man behind the wobbly looking table glared at her, tapping his fingers impatiently against the flat surface. Swallowing hard, she stepped forward.

He studied the top of her hat before slowly scrutinizing her, leaning over the table so he could see all the way down to the tips of her scuffed boots. With her brother's shirt and jacket, she was certain that none of her curves showed, nothing gave away the fact that she was a girl. But knowing and accepting were two different things. And no matter how she appeared, she still felt like a girl.

She clenched her jaws, trying to look as unfriendly as the fella standing against the wall did. Whatever it took to get hired, she'd do it.

"I'm Jake Vaughn. You got a name?" he asked gruffly as he settled back in his chair.

She nodded quickly.

"And it is?" he prodded.

She felt like such a fool. "S-Sam. Sam Reynolds."

"How old are you?"

"Sixteen."

He leaned forward. "Well, Sam, have you had any experience herding cattle?"

"Yes, sir," she answered quickly, comfortable with her answer. It wasn't a lie, exactly. She'd herded Old Bess out to pasture each morning and then back to the barn each evening.

He narrowed his eyes. "Why do I get the feeling you're lying to me?"

The fella standing against the wall shifted his stance slightly as though he was interested in her answer. Ignoring him, she focused all her attention on Mr. Vaughn.

"I ain't lying. I swear." With her finger, she made a cross over her heart. She almost repeated the childish refrain, "Cross my heart and hope to die . . ." but she figured a real cowboy wouldn't do that.

Slowly he looked her over one more time as though he was hoping to find some fault he might have missed the first time. Then he shook his head. "Sorry, Sam, but you're a little too scrawny."

Only he didn't look sorry at all. "But I'm strong," she insisted.

"Most of those fellas behind you are stronger. Sorry, son."

Sam's stomach dropped to the ground. She hadn't considered that he might tell her no. In the shadows of the night, with only the stars to wish on, her plan had seemed foolproof. She hadn't considered that a fool had come up with her plan.

"Move along now, son, we're burning daylight here," the man urged.

She almost snapped that she wasn't his son, wasn't anyone's son. Instead, she gathered her dignity together, thrust up her chin, and trudged away from the line of men and boys who would probably be hired.

She hadn't told her mother about her grand scheme because she hadn't wanted her mother to attempt to change her mind. She sought what comfort she could find in the fact that her family wouldn't be disappointed, wouldn't learn of her failure.

Her failure. Tears stung her eyes as she stormed down the alley between the buildings. She needed to be alone. Just for a few minutes. Before she headed home in disgrace.

Once behind the general store, she tore her hat from her head. "Dang it!" She kicked an empty crate. "Dang it!"

She'd shorn her hair and for what? For a foolish dream that would never happen. She kicked the crate again, taking no comfort in the echoing crack of splintering wood.

"Feeling better?" someone drawled.

She spun around, her heart hammering against her ribs. It was the young man who'd been staring at her while she'd been waiting in line. He was again leaning against a wall, his arms folded across his chest. Unlike her, he wasn't scrawny at all. Taller than she was, he had broad shoulders and a wide chest that tapered down to narrow hips. He was the type of person the trail boss wanted to hire, and that knowledge irritated her. "Don't you know it's rude to impose on a fella's misery?" she asked.

"Didn't mean to impose. Just thought maybe I could help you out."

"Not unless you got a herd to get to market and are lookin' to hire me," she said tartly as she crammed her hat back onto her head. Inwardly she scolded herself. It wasn't his fault that her dreams had been dashed and her hair was gone.

Sweeping his hat from his head, he squinted at the early morning sun. Her heart very nearly stopped. His eyes were a stunning blue. But it wasn't the color that snagged her attention as much as it was that he seemed to be a young man with an older man's eyes. A young man who had seen much that he might have wished he hadn't. A thin white scar creased his left eyebrow, parted the tiny black hairs there.

The scar made him seem mysterious, dangerous.

He leveled his gaze on her. Her stomach quivered.

"You shouldn't have lied to Jake," he said quietly.

Her breath caught. Somehow he'd managed to figure out she was a girl. Jake probably had as well. That was probably the real reason he hadn't hired her. Because he'd thought she was a scrawny girl.

"Telling him you knew how to herd cattle when you don't didn't sit too well with him," he added.

Relief swamped her with the realization that her secret was still safe, that he hadn't figured out anything of worth. She also realized that since he knew so much about Jake Vaughn, he must have worked with him for a while. He hadn't just been hired, as she'd thought. Envy speared her. To have the opportunity to earn a decent dollar . . . it just wasn't fair. "I *do* know how to herd cattle."

She grew uncomfortable under his harsh scrutiny as he captured her with his intimidating gaze.

"All right." She relented. "I know how to herd *one* cow. Our milk cow. To pasture and back."

His lips twitched, and for a heartbeat, she thought he was going to smile.

"It's not exactly the same," he said.

She jerked up her chin. "But I could learn."

"Why did you lie?"

"I need the hundred dollars. Bad. I'd do just about anything to be part of this outfit." And that was the honest-to-gosh-truth. "Besides, I'm a fast learner."

Nodding, he settled his black hat back into place. "The herd's camped about ten miles north of town. Just follow the road and you can't miss us. Report to Jake there at dawn tomorrow if you're serious about being part of the outfit."

Startled, she took a step back. He couldn't be saying what she thought he was saying. He couldn't be hiring her on. "But he said no," she reminded him.

"You just leave the trail boss to me. If you truly want the job, it's yours. Just don't ever lie again. We don't cotton to liars. If Jake finds out that you haven't been honest with him, he'll toss you on your butt and leave you to the vultures without giving you a penny. Understood?"

She nodded jerkily. She was going to lie during the entire journey . . . lie that she was a boy. As long as they didn't find out, where was the harm in her pretense? "Give you my word that I won't tell you another lie."

"And you're going to have to learn everything you need to know on your own. I've got no interest in being a teacher," he said.

Surely she could find an experienced cowhand who wouldn't mind taking a young boy under his wing and teaching him the ropes. And if she couldn't find one, she could learn by watching everyone carefully. How hard could trailing cattle truly be?

"I'll learn what I need without bothering you," she promised.

"Then we'll see you in the morning." He turned to leave.

"Wait!" she called out.

He glanced back at her over his shoulder.

"I-I don't even know your name."

"Matthew Hart."

Matthew Hart. He disappeared around the corner, and Sam sank to the ground as her legs finally gave out.

She'd actually done it. Somehow she'd managed to get hired to work on a cattle drive.

Now she just had to convince her mother to let her go.

Clank, clank, clank.

Leaning against the opening to the livery, Matthew Hart fought not to twitch every time the blacksmith pounded his hammer against the red-hot iron. Ever since the war, he was as skittish as a newborn colt whenever he heard a loud noise. Even when he was expecting the sound, his body did this quick jerk as though it was surprised by the commotion. It aggravated the daylights out of him.

Made him feel as though he was still a little kid instead of a man fully grown at eighteen. Although, truth be told, he figured he'd become a man at fourteen, when he'd marched into his first battle beating a drum to signal out the commanding officer's orders.

The roaring cannons and mortars had caused the ground to reverberate beneath his feet. He'd clutched the sticks he used to beat the drum so tightly that his knuckles had turned white. He thought he might have even cried the first time with the hail of bullets and the wailing of men surrounding him.

But there had been so much black smoke swirling around and dirt flying that if he had cried, no one had noticed. He figured a few of the older boys had probably been crying as well. War was a hell of a thing.

He remembered a time when he'd thought that tears were a sign of cowardice. Before the war ended, he would have sold his father's ranch just to be able to work up a solitary tear, to be able to feel anything except weary and eager to get home.

"Be just a few more minutes," the blacksmith said, snapping Matthew out of his reverie.

He nodded. "I'm in no hurry."

Hurry had no place on a cattle drive. They'd been moving the cattle up from the southern part of Texas for close to four weeks now. They were a couple of weeks shy of reaching Fort Worth.

Jake had heard rumors that the farmers in Kansas weren't too keen on cattle coming through. Some were sneaking into herds at night and starting stampedes. So Jake had decided to see if he could pick up a few extra hands.

If Matthew's horse hadn't thrown a shoe last night, he might never have had a chance to watch the trail boss hire the newest hands. Jake would have left him to tend the cattle.

Not that he would have minded. He was comfortable with the loneliness that crept over a man while he was watching a herd.

But then, if he'd stayed with the cattle, he wouldn't have spotted the kid.

He was having a difficult time understanding what had possessed him to follow the kid after Jake had dismissed him. Maybe it was because he reminded Matthew of the boys he'd come to know during the war. Frightened. Homesick. Pretending to be brave, hoping that if they convinced others, they could convince themselves. Boys like himself—growing up too dang fast, dying too dang young.

The boy had a face like so many others before their first battle: innocent looking, hopeful. Full of dreams that had yet to fade with the harshness of reality.

At the age of fifteen, when a mortar had blown his drum out of his hands, Matthew had picked up an abandoned rifle that he'd tripped over on the battlefield. From that moment on, he was no longer a drummer boy, but a soldier.

He'd fought in more battles than he cared to remember. Walked more miles than he wanted to think about. Been cold, wet, and hungry.

And so scared that even now the terror could creep up on him when he least expected it.

In the beginning, he'd been afraid that the war would end before he had a chance to fight.

Now he wished it had never started. And not just

because the South had lost, but because he felt as though he'd lost a part of himself as well.

No one else seemed to be aware of the truth that haunted him night and day.

The Matthew Hart who had returned home was not the same one who had gone off to war four years earlier. Carrying his dead friends off the battlefield had caused him to stop making friends. He'd rather bury strangers than someone he'd played cards with the night before. He preferred solitude, not getting close to anyone.

It made life less painful.

But the boy had looked so devastated after Jake's dismissal that Matthew had found himself trailing after him before he'd given much thought to what he was doing. He'd decided to reassure the boy that other opportunities to work a drive would come his way . . . not to be in such a hurry to grow up.

But then he'd seen the boy's frustrations as he'd kicked the crates . . .

Matthew understood the kid's feelings of helplessness, of having no control over his destiny. When the boy had turned around, tears welling in his eyes, his jaws clenched, he'd looked like a defeated soldier.

And Matthew had seen too damned many defeated soldiers, too many boys who were long past being helped.

So he'd offered the boy a place on the cattle drive. He could only hope that the kid wouldn't show up, but he doubted that was a possibility.

Matthew also knew the look of determination, and the kid had that as well.

Now all Matthew had to do was figure out how to break the news to Jake. And hope he wasn't fired in the process.

CHAPTER THREE

"Samantha Jane Reynolds, have you lost your ever-lovin' mind?"

Standing in the front room of the house, her pa's battered cowboy hat clutched in her hands, what was left of her hair curling around her face, Sam straightened her shoulders and squarely faced her mother. Cowering now would only give her mother ammunition that she could use to prove Sam had no business going on this cattle drive.

"It's a hundred dollars, Ma." She made her eyes grow big and round. "A hundred dollars. Think about what we could do with all that money."

"What I'm thinking about is what could happen to you on a cattle drive. You'd be the only young woman. It ain't right." Her mother shook her head. "It just ain't right."

"It's men and boys, Ma. And they think I'm a boy. I had a long talk with one fella. He was lookin' me over real close."

Almost as closely as she'd been looking him over. She couldn't figure out why she'd been unable to tear her eyes from him. Normally boys didn't hold her attention for long.

"He never figured out that I was a girl," she continued. "And I never aim to tell anyone, so I'll be fine. Besides, you let Benjamin go off to war when he was the same age as me," she pointed out.

"That's different. *He* was a *boy!*" her mother said.

"I can do this, Ma." She took a step closer. "Please, let me go. I promise I'll be all right."

"A promise is easily given, Samantha Jane, when you don't know what the future holds." Her ma cradled Sam's cheek. "I know you mean well, but all you're going to do is make me worry."

"Aren't you worried now, Ma? Don't you worry about how much more credit Mr. Thomas will give you at the general store? Don't you worry about the crops? How are you going to buy seed for next year? And Nate. He's growing. How are you gonna keep feeding him? By doing without enough food for yourself? Until you get sick, just like Pa?" She hadn't intended to be mean spirited with the reminder of her father, but she had to make her mother see the merits of letting Sam go on the cattle drive.

Her mother turned away. "We'll find a way."

"How, Ma? Just tell me how."

Her mother wiped her hands on the apron she

always wore. Patched now, it looked more like a tiny quilt. "I'll think of something."

But Sam heard the desperation in her mother's voice. "Benjamin won't go on this cattle drive because he doesn't think he can. I not only *think* I can, I *know* I can. Nate would do it, but he's not old enough. *I'm* old enough. I want to do this so badly that my chest aches when I think you might not let me. I know how to take care of myself."

Her mother faced her. Tears glistened in her eyes as she held out her arms. Sam stepped into her embrace, and her mother's arms closed around her.

"I keep forgetting that you grew up during the war," her mother rasped. "The money would be more than welcome and would sure go a long way toward making life easier." She leaned back and lovingly touched Sam's short curls. "Are you sure you want to do this?"

Sam nodded briskly. "I wouldn't have cut my hair otherwise, Ma. I'm not scared. It's a good outfit. It'll be an adventure."

Her ma hugged her close. "Then go with my blessings, and come home as soon as you can."

"You did what?"

Leaning against the tree, Matthew cut a quick glance at Jake Vaughn. "You're gonna start a stampede with all that bellowing, Jake."

He watched while Jake wore a path in the ground with his agitated pacing. Matthew had purposely waited until they'd returned to the herd to break his news. He hadn't wanted Jake to have time to track down the boy and inform him that Matthew had given him a false promise.

Jake stumbled to a stop. "He's a scrawny kid."

Matthew shrugged. "Just looked hungry to me. I've been hungry." More times than he cared to think about, when the Union had cut off their supplies. He didn't want to remember the things he'd eaten when nothing else was available. "Besides, he's got spunk."

Matthew thought about how the kid had jerked up his chin defiantly. Beneath the dirt, it didn't look like he was even growing whiskers yet. Heck fire, he'd probably lied about his age, too. He figured Jake had noticed that as well.

"He knows nothing about herding cattle," Jake pointed out.

"He can herd a milk cow."

"*A milk cow?* We've got two thousand head of cantankerous longhorns. Your pa hired me to get them to Sedalia."

Matthew rubbed the side of his nose and peered at Jake. "*My* pa, which in a way sort of makes this *my* herd." Even though his father had made it clear that Matthew wasn't to give orders; he was only to follow them. "Can't have two bosses," his father had explained.

This drive was the first one that they'd embarked on

since the war. Matthew had been raised around cattle, but he'd only been a kid when he'd helped his father herd them before the war. Trail bosses were paid well because they knew all there was to know about the cattle, the trail, and more important, about handling men. Matthew was still learning. He wasn't foolish enough to think he wasn't.

"Reckon I ought to have a say in who works for us," Matthew added. Although in truth, he knew he had no say whatsoever. If it came down to it, Jake could send him packing just as easily as he could the next man.

And considering the way Jake was glowering at him, he wouldn't be surprised if he did dismiss him right then and there.

Jake slowly nodded. "All right. We'll give the kid a chance to show us what he's made of. But if he lies to me one more time—"

"He won't," Matthew rushed to assure him. "I already warned him about your dislike for liars. You won't be sorry."

Jake took a threatening step toward him. "I promise you this, Matthew Hart. If I am? You'll be even sorrier."

Jake trudged off with his warning lingering in the air.

Matthew shifted his stance, wincing as he put unexpected pressure on his right leg. He'd taken a bullet at Gettysburg. His limp was barely noticeable now, although he found the twinges irritating.

But not as irritating as letting his father down by doing

something that would stop them from getting these cattle to market. He could only hope that he hadn't made the biggest mistake of his life by offering the boy a place on the drive.

He was still having a hard time believing that he'd interfered with the hiring. He'd always been one to follow orders—not interfere with them. Even when he disagreed with the man in charge, he did what he was told.

The boy would have to learn to do the same thing—without any help from Matthew.

He'd done his good deed for the day. From now on, the kid was on his own.

CHAPTER FOUR

As the sun eased over the horizon, blanketing the sky in various shades of orange and pink, Sam heard the cattle lowing as she urged Cinnamon off the main road and toward the rise. She was as nervous as a long-tailed cat curled up beneath a rocking chair. She'd stuffed a few precious belongings into a burlap sack and a saddlebag. She'd hugged her family good-bye before the sun had hinted at a new day. Since she hadn't slept a wink last night, she had been anxious to be on her way.

She guided her horse over the rise and the herd came into view. Cattle dotted the landscape, bathing it in shades of brown, russet, and chestnut. She tried not to contemplate what damage the steers' long horns might accomplish without much effort. These cattle were completely different from Old Bess. They looked fearsome and fearless.

She swallowed hard, trying to draw comfort from the knowledge that the cattle probably weren't that hard to manage, since the trail boss had apparently hired only a handful of cowboys to watch over them.

Sam guided her mare toward the wagon she spotted

in the distance. She wondered where Matthew was. As large as the herd was, she imagined the hands would have to spread out to keep the animals in line and stop them from wandering off. That tactic would work to her advantage. The more distance between her and the other hands, the better her chances of not having her secret discovered.

Of course, the harder it would be to learn all she needed to learn to carry her weight on this drive, and she was determined to do her part. The quicker she learned, the less dependent she'd be on anyone.

Matthew Hart had made it clear that he had no interest in teaching her, which was fine with her. He'd been kind to her yesterday, but she didn't want to be any more beholden to him. Besides, she needed to keep her distance to protect her disguise.

She brought her horse to a halt. A frumpy-looking man with white whiskers and a soiled apron was stacking pans in the back of the wagon. "Howdy!" she called out as she dismounted.

The man turned and glared at her. "You're too late. You want vittles, you git yourself here at five-thirty." He turned back to his chore.

He obviously thought she was already one of the cowhands—a fact she supposed boded well for her disguise. "Can you tell me where I'd find Mr. Vaughn?"

"I ain't his keeper," the grump tossed over his shoulder.

She fought not to feel dejected. Obviously she was going to be completely on her own here. Matthew Hart had no interest in her, and now, neither did this man. She assumed that was the way of a cowboy's life—having to do for oneself by oneself.

She turned her attention to the herd. She could see the cattle beginning to mill around and cowboys riding up and down the line. There were a lot more than those they'd hired in Faithful. She'd hung around the general store to make certain they didn't hire anyone she knew, anyone who might recognize her.

Judging by the number of men she'd seen them hire and the number she could spot now, they must have brought a passel of trail hands with them. She wondered if some had quit before they'd arrived in Faithful or if they'd just decided they needed extra hands. Regardless, Matthew had told her to be here at dawn and the sun was barely up.

She heard pounding hooves coming up behind her. She spun around. Her stomach tightened as Jake Vaughn and Matthew Hart neared. Sitting tall in the saddle caused them to strike imposing figures. She told herself that she would not allow them to intimidate her as they pulled back on the reins and brought their horses to a halt.

"Told you he'd show," Matthew said.

Mr. Vaughn reached into his pocket and tossed a coin toward Matthew, who caught it.

Matthew winked at her. "He bet me two bits you wouldn't come."

She didn't know why his wink made her feel as though they shared an intimate secret or why she found the slight curve of his lips intriguing. He wasn't looking at her the way that a boy looked at a girl in whom he had an interest. But she suddenly realized that she might be staring at him as a girl would . . . because it dawned on her with unexpected clarity that Matthew Hart was as handsome as sin.

His features were hard edged, as though they'd been chiseled by wind and sun. The lines in his face spoke of character and strength. And his eyes were so blue that she could easily drown in them.

She gave herself a mental shake and reined in her errant thoughts. She had to look at every man here as though she was a boy, the way Nate looked at Benjamin. As though with the least provocation she'd spit in his eye. She furrowed her brow to give herself a more serious demeanor.

"Told you I would. I keep my promises."

"Son, your voice hasn't even deepened its pitch. If you're sixteen—" Jake began.

"I *am* sixteen!" she interrupted, refusing to lose this opportunity to earn money. She swallowed hard. Too late to change her voice, so she'd have to fib a little. She promised herself this would be the absolute last lie. "It's just that the menfolk in my family tend to mature later than most."

Mr. Vaughn scowled. "Thought Matt explained to you about lying."

"He did." She drew an imaginary cross over her heart. "I swear I'm sixteen, Mr. Vaughn."

"Boss," he said.

"What?"

"The men who work for me call me boss."

She couldn't stop the smile from blossoming across her face. She was working for him! He might not have said that, exactly, but he'd sure implied it.

He jerked his thumb toward Matthew. "You'll ride beside Matt."

Her stomach dropped to somewhere around her knees with that declaration. She didn't want to ride beside Matt. He was too handsome, too distracting. She'd be better off riding beside some homely fellow and learning what she needed to from him.

Matthew obviously wasn't thrilled with the turn of events either, as his eyes widened. "Why does he have to ride with me?"

"Because you hired him, and you need to figure out what he knows and teach him what he doesn't know."

That answer seemed to irritate Matthew even more.

The last thing Sam wanted was to cause hardship for the one who'd helped her. "Can't he just tell me what I need to do, and then I can be on my own?"

Jake looked at her as though she was too ignorant to know not to question his orders. "No," he said in a voice that vibrated with warning. "Don't question my orders."

"Yes, sir," she replied meekly. She'd run the farm for so long that she'd almost forgotten what it felt like not to be the one in charge.

He looked at Matt. "You can both ride drag."

Matthew worked his jaw from side to side before asking, "Why do we have to ride *drag?*"

"So you'll learn not to hire someone without running it by me first." Jake turned his attention to Sam. "Cookie can store your gear in the supply wagon. Matt here will show you the ropes. I want you to stick to him closer than his shadow."

Not exactly where she wanted to be. She didn't want to be that close to anyone. The key to her success rested in her keeping her distance. Still, Sam nodded her understanding of the order and her gratitude for the opportunity to be part of the outfit. "You won't be sorry."

"You'd better hope I'm not, otherwise you'll be sorry as well. And Matt will be even sorrier." He turned his horse and rode off.

Her stomach tightened with the double warning.

She certainly didn't want to cause trouble for Matt.

Discreetly she peered at him. He looked as though he wanted to draw his gun from his holster and shoot the trail boss. His jaw was clenched tightly and his eyes were narrow slits of anger, a stormy blue that reminded her of turbulent waters.

She was determined to learn quickly so she could save both their positions with the outfit. "Is riding drag hard?"

He jerked his gaze to her as though he just now remembered she was there. He draped his wrist over his saddle horn. She shifted her stance beneath his intense scrutiny. With his thumb, he shoved his hat off his brow.

"It's not hard, but it's miserable. You end up choking down all the dust stirred up by the cattle. Hand your stuff over to Cookie, then mount up. The sooner we get started, the sooner you'll learn, and the sooner I can move back to point."

He made it sound as though riding point was better than riding drag. He was right. She did have a lot to learn. Including who everyone was.

"Who's Cookie?" she asked.

He tilted his head toward the supply wagon. "The cook. Most outfits call their cook Cookie."

"Why?"

He shrugged. "They just do. Come on, now, we're burning daylight."

She untied the burlap sack from around the saddle horn and cautiously approached the man who was now tying things into place at the wagon.

"My supplies," she offered. Such as they were.

He harrumphed, took them, and stuffed her bag in a corner in the back of the wagon.

"Appreciate it," she told him.

He grumbled something about "wet behind the ears" before turning away. Sam returned to her horse and pulled herself into the saddle.

Matt went to studying her again, making her feel like he might actually be wondering if she was a boy. She was confident that on the outside she resembled a boy, but on the inside she still felt like a girl. She didn't want to actually be a boy, but she needed to make sure she didn't act like a girl.

"Are we going or not?" she asked brusquely, knowing the less he looked at her, the less likely he was to figure out the truth about her.

"Have you got a bandanna?" he asked.

She noticed the red one that he'd tied loosely around his neck. She remembered that Jake had been wearing one as well. As a matter of fact, so had the cook. She shook her head. "No."

He reached into his saddlebag, withdrew one, and handed it to her. "You're gonna need one."

As soon as she took it, he pulled his own up over half his face, so his mouth and nose were covered. Following his example, she secured hers over her face and tied it behind her neck.

"You didn't want to ride drag?" she asked and her breath sent the bandanna fluttering over her face.

"No one wants to ride drag," he told her.

"So you're being punished for taking me on."

He shrugged haplessly. "Being reminded of my place in this outfit is more like it."

Her heart sank. It seemed she couldn't avoid being trouble for him, causing him hardship before they'd even gotten started. "I'm sorry."

"Don't be. Just become the best darn cowboy in the bunch so Jake will have to eat crow."

With that, he nudged his horse forward. Sam did the same, her excitement mounting. She was going on an honest-to-gosh cattle drive. An adventure . . . that had her shaking clear down to her boots.

As far as Matt was concerned, the only thing worse than riding drag was marching into battle. The cattle churned up enough dust to bury a man if he stood still for any length of time.

The prickly dirt and the smell of hide heated by the sun didn't seem to bother his riding partner any. The kid still sat with his back straight, his green eyes large and round as he peered over the bandanna as though he feared he'd miss out on something important. The boy reminded Matt too much of himself when he'd enlisted and trudged off to war. Before he'd experienced the hardships. Before he'd learned that war wasn't a game or an adventure or exciting.

Matt was going to hate watching this kid wilt as the day progressed toward night and his dreams gave way to the harsh reality of long, monotonous days.

If the kid was telling the truth about his age, then Matt was only two years older than Sam was. But he felt twenty years older. He felt as though he'd grown up and grown old at the same time. As though his youth had disappeared down a bottomless well.

He certainly couldn't remember a time when he'd been bouncing in the saddle with eagerness—anxious to see what waited around the corner. It was wearing him out just watching the kid's energy.

"How many cattle are there?" Sam suddenly asked.

It occurred to Matt that the boy might have been sitting up so straight because he'd been trying to count the cattle, but they were stretched out for several miles.

"Little over two thousand," Matt answered.

"What does the marking on the cattle stand for? It looks like the top and bottom part of a heart, spread apart," the boy said.

The kid was observant. Matt had to give him credit for paying attention. But the kid's youth revealed itself with his eagerness, his questions.

"That's exactly what the brand is. A broken heart. These cattle belong to the Broken Heart ranch," he explained.

"That's such a sad name for something. Why is it called that?"

Matt shook his head. Yeah, it was a sad name for a sad tale. Most cowboys just took the symbol of the brand and the name of the ranch at face value.

"I'll tell you the long, boring story later. Too much trail dust out here."

His light green eyes sparkling with anticipation, Sam looked at Matt and nodded. Nothing seemed to dim the kid's enthusiasm. Not the heat, the flies, the boredom.

He reminded Matt of other boys he'd known. Maybe they were the reason Matt had gone after Sam the day before.

Because he'd reminded Matt of the friends he'd been unable to save.

And now he reluctantly had this kid in his care. What had he been thinking to take Sam on?

He'd thought Jake would be responsible for the young cowhand. He should have figured the task of teaching the boy would fall to him.

He'd followed orders, was so danged good at following orders—even when he didn't agree with them. And because of his dogged determination to obey commands during the war, the boys in his command had suffered. Many had even died.

It was now his goal to make sure Sam didn't join them.

CHAPTER FIVE

The sun was directly overhead when Sam noticed the cattle starting to slow down—if beasts that barely moved could be said to slow down. She thought they'd be lucky if they covered fifteen miles today.

All morning she and Matt had simply ridden behind the beasts, keeping a watchful eye. Every now and then, Matt would urge his horse toward an errant cow. He used his rope, coiled but dangling loosely from his hand, to shoo the animal back toward the herd. He'd shown her how to hold her own rope, how to gently flap it to direct the animals.

The work wasn't hard, but it was tiresome. And so dull that she couldn't figure out why Mr. Vaughn hadn't been willing to hire her in the first place. As far as she could tell, the greatest danger was falling asleep and toppling off her horse.

The cattle came to a stop. Two cowboys loped toward them and brought their horses to a halt.

"We'll take first shift," one said.

"You'll get no argument from me," Matt responded. "Sam, meet Jeb and Jed."

Sam couldn't tell much about them, since their hats shielded the top of their heads and their bandannas hid the lower part of their faces. She could see that they both had tawny eyes.

"They're twins," Matt explained. "If you can't remember which is which, just call out, 'Twin.' They both answer to that."

"How come you're riding drag, instead of point, like you have been?" one twin asked.

"Gotta teach Sam the *ropes*, so to speak," Matt told him tersely, "and the boss wouldn't let him start at the front."

Guilt pricked Sam's conscience. Matt had explained the various positions to her. Farther up were the cowboys who rode flank. Ahead of them, the cowboys were riding the swing position. Point was obviously a coveted spot, in front of the herd, ahead of the choking dust. Matt had been forced to give it up because he'd offered her a spot on this drive.

She would definitely do all she could to become the best cowhand Jake Vaughn or Matthew Hart had ever seen. Or die trying.

"Come on, Sam. Cookie will have set up the wagon at the front of the herd and we have about an hour before we get these little doggies moving again. And we'll need to get back here so Jeb and Jed can have a chance to eat."

Following Matt's lead, she urged her horse into a canter.

She couldn't remember the last time she'd been this hungry.

Matt had explained that the wagon started out ahead of the herd and traveled to a spot that Jake had determined the night before. When Cookie reached it, he set up and prepared lunch. The meal was usually ready by the time the slow-moving cattle caught up to him. He'd follow the same plan during the afternoon. Where Cookie stopped late in the afternoon was where they'd stay for the night.

As they approached the noonday camp, she could see several cowboys squatting near the supply wagon, shoveling food into their mouths.

She dismounted. Matt took the reins to her mare and tethered it to a nearby bush near his horse.

"Go on and get yourself some food," he ordered.

She cautiously walked toward the cook. He was dipping a ladle into a huge Dutch oven and bringing out stew.

"I'll have some, please," she said.

He turned the ladle to the side to unload its contents. Juice splattered the bowl as the stew hit it. "Son-of-a-gun," he said.

"That's all right," she told him. "It didn't make too much of a mess."

He scrunched up his face, and she could have sworn the white whiskers on his face bristled. "I was tellin' you the name of the stew. It's son-of-a-gun stew."

"Oh." She smiled slightly. "I've never heard of that

kind of stew. What's in it?"

"Whatever was easiest to reach."

She didn't think that sounded too appetizing. She took the bowl and headed for a nearby tree. She thought about sitting with the other cowboys, but she decided that the less time she spent in their company, the less likely they were to discover she was a girl.

Gingerly she brought a spoonful of stew to her lips and tentatively touched the tip of her tongue to the sauce. Not bad. Not like anything she'd ever tasted before, but not bad.

Out of the corner of her eye, she saw Matt take his bowl and drop down beside the wagon, pressing his back to the wooden wheel. She figured he was just as happy to be away from her for a while as she was to be avoiding him. He hadn't been unkind during their time together, but he hadn't exactly been friendly, either.

She'd just finished the last of her stew when Jake crouched in front of her. She hadn't seen him come into camp. She was wishing he hadn't seen her. He was holding a length of rope about two feet long. He extended it toward her.

"Take it and tie a knot for me," he ordered.

Licking her lips, she set the bowl aside, took the rope, and expertly tied a knot at its center. Nodding, Jake took the rope and jerked the ends, tightening her knot.

"That's a knot all right," he murmured.

She started to smile at passing his test, but he sliced

his gaze to her and his harsh scrutiny caused her smile to wither.

"Can you do a double half-hitch?" he asked.

She slowly shook her head.

"Clove hitch?"

Again she shook her head, wishing she hadn't eaten her stew so quickly. Her stomach was starting to hurt as she realized she hadn't impressed him in the least.

"They're one and the same," he told her. "We use them to secure our horses because the knots can be untied quickly. If a horse tugs on the rope with your kind of knot, it's just going to tighten and you'll never get it loose."

"Cinnamon is trained not to run off."

"I don't care how well your horse is trained, it's gonna bolt if two thousand cattle are running. Besides, you're not always going to ride your horse. We've got horses trained for night riding. And we have cow ponies that will serve you better when you give your horse a rest. Matt!"

She snapped her head back, astounded by his abrupt yelling of Matt's name. Apparently Matt was equally startled, because she saw his body jerk and his bowl went flying. She might have laughed at his reaction if Jake hadn't had her pinned to the spot with his stare.

Glowering, Matt got to his feet, picked up his bowl, handed it to Cookie, and trudged toward them.

"What?" he asked when he got near enough to be heard without yelling.

Jake unfolded his body and tossed the rope at Matt. Matt caught it.

"He doesn't know how to tie any other kind of knot except that one. Teach him," Jake commanded.

Matt rolled his eyes. "Jake, you're being unreasonable."

"Me? I'm not the one who hired him. Teach him or fire him. It's your choice."

Sam's heart slammed against her ribs. Half a day? He was only going to give her half a day to prove herself?

With long strides, Jake walked away. Matt dropped his head back and closed his eyes. Sam could almost see the battle he waged within himself. She had an uncomfortable feeling that teaching her wasn't winning out over firing her. When he'd offered to hire her, he obviously hadn't realized he'd be responsible for her. But then she hadn't realized that, either.

"I'm a fast learner," she said quickly.

With a deep sigh, he opened his eyes and looked at her. "Let's hope so."

He hunkered down in front of her. She watched as his fingers worked to untie her tightened knot. He'd removed his gloves to eat, and she could see now that he had long, tanned fingers.

His hands looked much stronger than hers. His veins stuck up like tiny mountain ranges. When he turned his hands, the calluses became visible. She couldn't imagine why she was so fascinated by the movement of his fingers and hands. She'd never spent much time noticing a boy's hands or the firmness in his forearms.

But sitting here with Matt, watching him work, she thought he had the most capable hands she'd ever seen. She wondered what it would feel like to have his hand wrapped around hers, their palms pressed together.

"How many different kinds of knots are there?" she asked, trying to rein in her wandering thoughts.

"About a half dozen that we use," he answered distractedly. He tugged the rope straight, the knot gone, before lifting his gaze to hers. "Spanish, rose, double half-hitch, square, hackamore, granny, half." His wide shoulders rolled as he shrugged. "We'll do one a day until you've learned them all. We'll start with a square knot. Now watch."

She did. She really did like the way his hands moved, so capable, so sure. She never would have thought she'd find that one aspect of a man incredibly engrossing. He had to show her three times before she remembered to watch the rope and not his fingers.

When he gave the rope to her, she took a deep breath and mimicked his actions. She held up the square knot.

He smiled then, a smile that reached up to touch his blue eyes and made them sparkle like jewels dangling from a necklace. "Impressive. Let's get back to the herd so Jed and Jeb can come eat. Bring the rope. You can practice a bit as long as the cattle stay calm."

She got to her feet. "Thanks, Matt."

He nodded before he sauntered away, leaving her to feel as though once again there was something she either didn't know or had failed to do properly.

And yet she couldn't help but feel that he was more upset with himself than with her. He always seemed to start out impatient, but as he explained things he actually became . . . friendly.

Then he'd back off as though he'd stepped across an invisible line he'd never planned to get near. She didn't quite know what to make of him or his attitude.

She understood that he didn't want to ride drag. But she had the feeling that she was the true thorn in his side. And she couldn't figure out why.

CHAPTER SIX

The kid's gratitude nagged at Matt's conscience. Hiring the boy had been a stupid idea. Softening his heart toward him was even stupider. If Matt had any kindness in him, he'd send the kid home before they traveled much farther.

The problem was that Sam had such innocent eyes . . . and Matt didn't want to be the one who tore that innocence asunder, who taught the boy that life was difficult and growing up was hard. Giving Sam less than a day to prove himself would surely do that.

Sam had looked at Matt as though he was some kind of hero for teaching him how to tie a square knot. And he was a far cry from being a hero.

He cast a sly glance Sam's way as his horse plodded along. He'd decided to teach the kid another knot, and Sam was now busily working to master the double half-hitch. The kid had such small hands—delicate, almost. Jake was right. Sam wasn't anywhere close to being sixteen.

Closer to fourteen, maybe even younger. Why lie about his age when they were hiring fourteen-year-olds?

Obviously the kid wanted to grow up, and grow up fast.

Sam's slight build made Matt want to protect him, protect him the way he'd tried to protect boys younger than him during the war—and that was a dangerous undertaking on a cattle drive.

Every man had to be capable of caring for himself, and the sooner Matt taught Sam all he needed to know, the sooner Matt could stop worrying about him. He hated worrying about someone else almost as much as he hated riding drag.

During the war, the soldiers kept getting younger and younger. He'd been promoted to lieutenant at sixteen because he'd been the oldest in the outfit. He'd thought that had been a fairly pitiful reason to put him in charge. Sometimes he thought the war was more of a boys' war than anything else.

And cattle drives were becoming no different. So many men had gone off to fight. The youngsters left behind had started herding cattle. They were the reason that trail hands were now referred to as *cowboys*.

Matt fought an inner battle not to worry about Sam. He'd teach him what he needed to learn, and the boy would do fine. He had spoken the truth about his ability to learn quickly.

Matt turned his attention back to the herd. He supposed it wouldn't hurt to be a little nicer to the kid. Sam rarely spoke so Matt didn't have to worry that the boy would try to develop a friendship with him. There were dangers on a cattle drive—not as many as a man found at war, but enough that it wasn't uncommon to lose a man or two. If Matt kept his distance, it wouldn't hurt so much if someone did die on him.

He'd do one favor for Sam, just to ease his own guilt for not really wanting Sam around. Then he could go back to just teaching him what he needed to learn and avoiding him the rest of the time.

Sam had plowed fields, planted seed, harvested crops, hunted game, mended fences, worked from dawn till dusk. She had expected sitting astride a horse all day, trailing cattle to be easy.

It had been anything but. She was covered in dust from head to toe. And bored out of her ever-loving mind. In spite of the thick clouds churned up by the plodding hooves, she'd tried to strike up a conversation or two with Matt, but he seemed reluctant to speak more than a couple of words at time. He had a habit of quickly putting a halt to her attempts by telling her they'd discuss it later.

Which was probably for the best.

Every time she practiced tying a knot, she'd think about his hands and wonder what their touch might feel like.

She didn't understand why her thoughts kept wandering to images of her and Matt together—together with him knowing she was a girl. Smiling at her. Holding her hand.

None of the boys who had returned from the war had made her realize that she was truly growing up, that she was beginning to have a woman's dreams. She thought she might even be interested in attending a dance if Matt was going to be there.

Where were all these strange ideas coming from? Was this the way Mary Margaret felt every time she got near Benjamin? Did her heart pound, her palms get damp, and her mouth grow dry?

Sam wondered if all this was indeed the result of an attraction to Matt. She sure hoped she wasn't on the verge of getting sick, for surely Jake would send her home if she wasn't feeling well.

The cattle began to slow much as they had around noon.

Matt moved his hand in a circle. "We're gonna start moving them in closer to each other, preparing to bed them down for the night." He nodded toward the west. "Be twilight soon, and we can relax a little."

Relax. She thought of relaxing at home, sitting before the hearth, curled up with a good book. Her family owned only six, but she never tired of reading them. She always noticed something new in the story, some small thing she might have overlooked the first time.

It took them close to an hour to get the herd settled. At the camp, Sam turned Cinnamon over to the wrangler who would see to the horse's needs until Sam needed the mare for her watch later that evening.

Standing beside her, Matt pulled his bandanna down. Dirt was embedded within the creases of his face and the corners of his eyes, but the bandanna had done its job well and kept the lower portion of his face safe from dust. Sam smiled brightly.

"What's so funny?" he asked.

"You look like a pesky raccoon."

"I can be downright pesky when I want to be. Guess I was this morning when I found out that I had to ride with you. Come on, I'll make it up to you."

He took off at a fast clip. She fell into step beside him. "Where are we going?"

"To relax a little, like I promised."

They wended their way through the thick copse of oak trees.

"What did you think of herding cattle?" Matt tossed over his shoulder.

"It was fun."

Matt stopped in his tracks and faced her, boring his gaze into hers. When he wasn't angry, he had the prettiest eyes, with long, dark lashes sweeping around them. For a minute, Sam wished she wasn't wearing her brother's old shirt and britches. She wished she were wearing a pretty dress. Only if she were, he'd figure out in a heartbeat that she was a girl.

"Truthfully," he prodded.

She exhaled. "Kinda boring."

His mouth did that little quiver as though he was contemplating grinning, but couldn't quite bring himself to do it.

"That's the cattle business. Days of boredom, interspersed with a few minutes of excitement." He continued trudging forward.

"When do we get the excitement?" Sam asked.

"When the cattle stampede."

Faltering, she almost tripped over an exposed root. "Stampede?"

"Yep. Longhorn cattle stampede at just about anything: twig snapping, lightning flashing, thunder rolling. It doesn't take much. When that happens, you just ride the perimeter and stay out of their way."

When? Not if. "You ever been on a trail drive when they *didn't* stampede?"

"Nope."

He came to a halt. Beyond him, a river flowed. The shade from the trees lining the bank rested gently on the brown water. She watched in amazement as he unbuttoned his shirt and pulled it off. He had broad shoulders. The muscles across his bronzed chest rippled with his movements.

Lifting a foot, he hopped while he pulled off a boot. "Come on," he ordered.

"Come on?" she repeated.

He tugged off the other boot. "Get your clothes off."

Before she knew what he intended, he shucked off his britches, baring his backside and anything else she cared to look at. Sam spun around, her cheeks flaming with the heat of embarrassment. Her breath came in short little gasps.

"What's wrong?" he asked.

She shook her head wildly. When Nate was small, she used to help her mother give him a bath. But her younger brother certainly didn't resemble Matt. Matt's body was that of a man, not a baby. And there was a world of difference between the two.

"Are you modest?" Matt asked, clearly baffled by her behavior.

When she didn't answer, he laughed. Actually laughed. His low-pitched rumble echoed between the trees, circled on the breeze, touched her heart. How long had it been since she'd heard laughter?

"Sam, you haven't got anything that I don't have."

That was certainly a lie, and she had no plans to correct his false assumption.

"I figured you'd enjoy a swim after trailing in the dust all day," he added.

She'd love a swim, but not when it meant removing her clothes. Or staring at him in his birthday suit. Because if she did look at him, she'd surely stare at a sight she'd never before seen.

"Whoowee!" someone yelled from the thicket before four young men came running out from between the trees.

"Been waiting all day for this!" Jed yelled. Or was it Jeb?

Sam didn't know. She only knew that they were stripping off their clothes as quickly as Matt had.

"Sam, say howdy to Slim and Squirrel," Matt ordered. "They ride flank."

Only she couldn't say anything. The knot in her throat wouldn't even let her swallow.

"What's wrong with the greenhorn?" Slim asked.

"I think he's a tad modest. Sam, haven't you ever gone skinny dipping?" Matt asked.

Without answering, she rushed back through the trees toward camp, with their laughter echoing around her. *Escape!* screamed through her mind. *Run, run* echoed with each step she took.

She heard the splashes as the young men apparently

jumped into the river. Jumped in as naked as the day they were born.

She tripped over a gnarled root and landed hard on the ground. Twigs and dried leaves scraped her palm and skinned her knee. She pushed herself to her feet and hurried on. She'd never expected that boys would be so . . . so bold.

Only they didn't know they were being bold because they didn't know they had a female in their midst. They simply thought she was one of them—which was exactly what she wanted them to believe. Only she wanted their clothes to remain on their bodies!

Slowing her step, she finally came to a halt, sank to the ground, and leaned her back against a tree. Her harsh breathing made her chest ache.

She heard pounding footsteps, and then Matt was crouched before her. He was wearing his britches now, but he hadn't taken time to put on his boots. His bare toes were curled into the dirt. Little sprigs of hair dotted his big toe. It seemed incredibly intimate to be staring at a man's toes.

She lifted her gaze and realized toes weren't nearly as personal as his chest, heaving with each labored breath he took. She watched a solitary drop of sweat roll into the hollow at the center of his bared chest.

"Sam?"

She jerked her gaze up to his, to those mesmerizing blue eyes. His knitted brow reflected his concern. Dark locks of his hair had fallen over his forehead. Without thinking, she started to raise her hand to brush them aside, to see if they felt as silky as they looked.

"It's all right, Sam," he said quietly. "I know your secret."

CHAPTER SEVEN

Sam looked downright terrified as all the blood rapidly drained from his face, leaving him looking stark white against the dark bark.

"How—how did you figure it out?" Sam stammered.

"It's just so incredibly obvious."

"But what . . . what did I do that gave the truth away?"

It hurt to hear the absolute panic in Sam's voice.

"It's all right, Sam," Matt said quietly. "Jake won't make you leave."

Disbelief marred Sam's face. "Yes, he will."

"No, he won't. A lot of the fellas can't swim."

The kid looked to Matt as though he'd just swallowed a June bug. "Swim?" Sam rasped.

Matt nodded. At the creek, the boy's cheeks had flamed red, burning so brightly that Matt figured he could have started a fire with them. Matt had never seen a fella react in that manner before.

He'd remembered the first time he'd shucked his clothes in the army. He'd been a little self-conscious, standing there in the altogether with men he barely knew, but he'd figured it wasn't that much different from skinny dipping with his friends in the creek back home.

The kid had looked as though he'd never caught sight of a naked body before. He'd looked . . . well . . . afraid. That had made no sense to Matt unless Sam did fear something. Then it had hit Matt like a bolt of lightning: the boy was afraid of the river. To be afraid like that could mean only one thing—the boy didn't know how to swim.

Sam had some pride. Maybe too much. He'd certainly shown it the day before, behind the general store.

"I could teach you, if you want," Matt offered. He didn't particularly want to, but neither did he want the kid drowning on him.

The boy still looked ready to bolt at any minute.

Sam shook his head. "Nah, nah . . . I've got a powerful fear of the water."

Matt grimaced and rubbed the side of his nose. That was the last thing he wanted to hear. "What are you going to do when we get to the Red River and have to swim the cattle across?"

"As long as I can stay on my horse, I'll be fine."

But Matt had seen more than one cowboy fall off his horse crossing a river. And he had seen many a cowboy drown. "I think you ought to let me teach you to swim."

"Nah, I'll be fine, I swear it."

"All right, then, but when we get to the Red, you stick close to my side, where I can see you at all times."

"I will."

Matt heard the clanking of iron that meant Cookie had the vittles ready. "Go on and eat. We'll be watching the cattle at midnight."

Sam struggled to his feet and Matt unfolded his tall, lean body.

"You won't tell no one, will you? 'Bout my secret?" Sam asked.

"No."

"Give me your word that you won't tell a soul."

"I give you my word, Sam, but it's nothing to be ashamed of."

"I know. I just don't want the other fellas making fun of me."

"They'd have to deal with me if they did." Now, why had he said that? He wasn't supposed to be protecting Sam. He was supposed to be teaching the kid to take care of himself. He tugged Sam's hat down over his eyes. "Go on, get."

Leaning against the tree, he watched as Sam hightailed it back to camp. Matt had never had a younger brother, but he sure felt like an older brother to Sam. The boy just seemed amazingly wary of things, incredibly afraid of doing wrong. He wished he knew how to give the boy confidence. His lack of faith in himself seemed at odds with his spunk.

Matt turned back toward the river. He'd just take a

quick dunk now, anything to wash away the memory of the terror he'd seen in Sam's pale green eyes.

He was glad the kid didn't want to take swimming lessons. Matt didn't want to be an older brother to the boy. He didn't even want to be a friend. It hurt too much to lose a friend.

It had been a mistake to bring Sam to the river. Not because he couldn't swim, but because just for a moment as the kid had trailed along behind him, Matt had enjoyed his company, had forgotten that the last thing he wanted was a friendship.

As soon as she finished eating supper, Sam grabbed her bedroll out of the back of the supply wagon and moved a good distance away from the campfire, away from where it appeared the other cowhands were bedding down for the night. As she smoothed her bedroll over the ground, she fought back the images of Matt's bared body, but it was a battle she kept losing.

Matt had frightened ten years off her earlier this evening with his proclamation. "I know your secret."

Her heart had very nearly stopped. She'd thought he'd figured out that she was a girl.

She could only be grateful that he'd attributed her hasty retreat to an inability to swim and not to her embarrassment at standing there dumbfounded, staring at his white backside and hairy calves. And thighs that looked as though they'd been chiseled from stone, although stone not as dark as the rock used for his chest.

She'd never in her life imagined that a man could look . . . beautiful. She'd remember the sight of Matt outlined by the twilight shadows for as long as she drew breath.

She could swim—in truth, she loved the water—but she couldn't enjoy it without giving away her true reason for reacting as she had. Besides she didn't figure Matt or any of the other cowboys would appreciate knowing that they'd removed their clothes in front of a girl.

She sat on her pallet, squirming to get comfortable. It seemed every time she removed a rock from beneath her bedroll, another showed up to take its place. She glanced toward the fire burning brightly in the center of the camp. Several hands were sitting near it, including Matt.

The others were laughing and talking. Matt was simply staring at the writhing flames, his hands clasped around a tin cup. She wondered what he was thinking about, how he could appear to be separate from the others even though he was sitting beside them.

She drew her knees up to her chest and wrapped her arms around them, holding them tightly. Matt wasn't wearing his hat. His black hair brushed the collar of his shirt. The desire to touch it earlier had taken her by surprise. She couldn't recall ever wanting to touch a boy's hair.

What was happening to her? Why was she noticing things about Matt—the thickness of his hair, the strength in his hands, the deep timbre of his voice, the rumble of his laughter, the incredible blue of his eyes—that she'd never paid attention to before when it came to boys?

She tried to tell herself that she was fascinated with Matt just because she'd known so few boys in the past four years. But if it was simply a matter of Matt being a boy, why couldn't she remember the color of the twins' eyes? Why did she have to look at Squirrel to remember his hair was brown and at Slim to know his hair was blond?

Why did it seem like every facet of Matt had been branded on her mind so she could see him clearly every time she closed her eyes?

She told herself it was because she'd been forced to spend the entire day in his company. But a secret corner of her heart echoed that she was lying to herself.

If she'd never seen Matthew Hart again after yesterday morning, she would have remembered him to her dying day.

She snapped her head around as Jake knelt beside her.

"Set yourself up kinda far from the others," he said quietly.

Sam nodded, stalling for time while she decided how to explain herself without lying or causing suspicion. She thought she'd be as uncomfortable sleeping beside one of the cowboys as she'd been seeing them at the river this afternoon. Besides, she thought it best to keep her distance as often as she could. "I'm not used to sleeping with a bunch of men and boys."

Inwardly she smiled. That was the truth.

"A lot of these fellas snore, but most of us are too tired to notice, once our head hits the ground." He'd planted his elbows on his thighs and was balanced on the balls of his feet as though at any moment he thought he might have to get up. "Cattle are more likely to stampede at night. What will you do if they start running?"

He was studying her like she was supposed to know the answer. She shook her head slightly and tried to remember what Matt had told her earlier. In a timid voice, she said, "Ride the perimeter and stay out of their way?"

He twisted his body slightly and looked over his shoulder. "Matt!"

Sitting near the fire, Matt jerked as though he was a puppet and someone had yanked on his strings.

Slowly Matt rose to his feet and stalked across the camp. "Dang it, Jake, stop hollering at me."

"You seem a bit skittish today."

"I was lost in thought, that's all." He crouched beside Jake and darted a glance at Sam before giving his full attention to Jake. "What did you need?"

"Sam doesn't know the particulars of what to do during a stampede."

"I'll explain the details to him before I turn in."

"Is that your sleeping gear on the other side of the camp?"

Matt narrowed his eyes, and Sam wondered if he was

considering lying. She had a bad feeling that neither one of them was going to like where Jake was heading with his question.

"Yeah, it is," Matt said slowly.

"Gather it up. You're sleeping beside Sam tonight."

With a groan, Matt dropped his head back. "Jake, the kid's been dogging my heels all day. We can use a little time apart. Nothing is gonna happen."

"Know that for a fact, do you?" Jake asked.

Matt sighed. "I know you ordered Sam to stay as close to me as my shadow, but *you know* that I sleep away from the camp."

"Should have thought of that before you hired him. Either stick to him like stink on manure, or send him home. If I have to tell you again, I'll send *you* home." Jake got to his feet. "I mean it, Matt. Stop shirking your responsibilities where the kid is concerned."

Sam watched Matt's jaw move back and forth, the muscles in his face tight as he glared at Jake's retreating back.

"Get up," he ground out through clenched teeth.

"Why?"

"We're going into the woods. I've got business to tend to."

Sam's eyes widened. "Oh, no, Matt, I'm sure Jake didn't mean I had to follow you when you needed to take care of nature's call."

The last thing she wanted to do was intrude on his privacy.

"Follow me, or pack up and go home," he ordered.

"You sound just like Jake."

"Don't I, though?"

He lunged to his feet and stormed into the thicket of trees. He was contrary and confusing. He'd been kind and considerate after she'd run from the river, and now he was issuing ultimatums. She didn't understand him. Nice one minute, ornery the next. If she didn't need that money . . .

Sam waited only a heartbeat before bolting after him.

CHAPTER EIGHT

It wasn't nature's call that Matt needed to deal with; it was his frustrations. Why was he being punished? He couldn't figure that part out as he wended his way through the trees.

Out of the kindness of his heart, he'd offered the kid a place on the drive . . . and Jake was bound and determined to make him regret his actions.

Made no sense. Made no sense at all.

Why did he have to stick to Sam like flies on cow dung?

He reached the river and started pacing its bank. He considered saying to hell with it and heading home, but if he did that, then Jake would surely let the kid go. So his going wouldn't accomplish anything except to leave Jake short two hands instead of one. He was contemplating the merits of sending the boy home himself when Sam joined him at the river's edge.

The kid was out of breath and rubbing his hands up and down his thighs, obviously as nervous as a June bug in a chicken coop.

Matt dropped his head back and plowed his hands through his hair. He couldn't bring himself to send the kid packing, not when he looked at Matt as though he hung the stars.

"I . . . I don't snore," the boy said.

He stopped pacing, raked his fingers through his hair one more time, turned, and faced the kid. "It's not that I'm worried about you snoring. I'm just used to . . . sleeping kinda off by myself."

Even in the moonlight, he could see the kid scrunching up his face. "You do a lot of things by yourself."

"No, I don't."

The boy took a brazen step forward. "Yes, you do. You eat over by the supply wagon—"

"Why carry my food a good distance away when I can just eat it there and hand the plate back to Cookie?" That was a sorry excuse if ever he heard one. Friendships developed during meals and he had no need of friends.

Sam shook his head. "I think there's more to it than that. At the fire, you were sitting close enough to make it look like you were part of the group, but you weren't really listening to what they said. And you jump every time Jake yells at you."

"Who wouldn't? He's got a voice as loud as thunder."

As loud as the retort of a rifle or the boom of a cannon.

"You don't strike me as someone who normally would jump."

"Yeah, well, shows what you know."

He turned away and looked out over the river,

disgusted that he sounded as young as the kid. He could hear the water lapping against the shore, a fish splashing somewhere. Frogs croaked and crickets chirped.

He didn't want to spend time with the kid. If he did, he might come to care for him . . . if Sam drowned crossing the river or got trampled during a stampede or got bitten by a snake or got struck by lightning. Lord have mercy . . . the dangers were endless.

And when someone you cared about died, it hurt. It hurt something fierce, as though a part of you was dying as well. He'd learned during the war to shut the door on his emotions. To stop caring.

Why did this kid have to make him feel like an older brother? Worse, why did he make him *want* to be an older brother, to take him under his wing and help him? To show Jake that Matt was a good judge of character?

He spun around and the kid leapt back. "All right. Here's how it's gonna be. You're gonna do just like Jake said and stick closer to me than my shadow. You're gonna do everything that I say, exactly as I say . . . and you're gonna stop watching me so closely."

"How am I supposed to stop watching you if I'm right beside you all the time?"

"Figure something out. We're not going to be friends or blood brothers—"

"I didn't ask you to be anything to me. Why are you angry at me?"

"I'm not angry." But he realized he sounded angry. He sighed. "Look, Sam, when I hired you on, I hadn't planned on having to spend every minute of every day and night with you. I'm trying to make the best of a bad situation."

Sam nodded brusquely. "Fine. Just teach me what you need to. I can be as unfriendly as you."

Matt saw the boy spin on his heel and start walking away.

"Hold on, kid. You can't go back to camp until I'm ready. Jake's orders."

Sam stopped, and Matt watched as the boy crossed his arms over his chest.

Matt could sense the boy glaring at him through the darkness. He didn't know why he was being so ornery where Sam was concerned. The kid hadn't asked Matt to be his friend. Matt was the one who kept interfering, sticking his nose where it didn't belong, trying to save the boy. When was he going to learn that people couldn't be saved? That no matter what you did, in the end, nothing made a difference?

He stepped forward. "All right, we can go."

"I don't like this any better than you do," Sam grumbled.

Sam tried to ignore the quiver in her stomach as Matt dropped his bedroll beside hers and crouched. She knew sleeping beside him wasn't going to be anything like sleeping beside Amy.

Amy wasn't muscular. Matt looked as though he'd never been a stranger to hard work. Amy smelled of violets. Matt smelled of horses and leather.

Amy didn't have a beard shadowing her face. Neither did she move with a rhythm that said she'd bedded down beneath the stars a hundred times before.

Sam ran her fingers through her shorn curls. She stilled once she realized she was primping. Why did she feel the need to look presentable? She was supposed to be a boy, not a girl vying for Matt's attention.

Matt toed off his boots. At least he was wearing socks now, but she couldn't quite forget how his bare feet had looked. The sleeves on his shirt were rolled up to his elbows, exposing the corded muscles of his forearms.

Matt tugged his shirttail loose from his britches, stretched out on the ground, and folded his arms beneath his head. A couple of his buttons popped loose from their holes, and Sam could see his chest. So remarkably different from hers.

Although his chest looked hard, she imagined it would be comforting to press her cheek against it. To have him tell her that she wasn't crazy to be on this drive. Turning her back to him, she settled onto her side, curling her knees toward her stomach.

She didn't need to be thinking about cuddling up against Matthew Hart. She couldn't fathom why she wanted to. She'd never before yearned to be held by a boy. Before the war, she had enjoyed racing against them, climbing trees with them, outsmarting them, and ignoring them when the mood struck.

She was having a heck of a time ignoring Matt. Every time she closed her eyes, she saw him stretched out in that inviting pose. She could see herself rolling over and fitting against his side. His arm coming down to wrap her protectively in his embrace.

She squirmed. She certainly didn't need those thoughts.

She could hear the flames crackling in the campfire, the distant lowing of the cattle, the slight breeze rustling the leaves in the trees. It was all so calming, incredibly peaceful.

A thousand stars blanketed the night sky. A full moon poured its pale light over the landscape. And a young man she couldn't seem to stop thinking about was sleeping beside her. She wiggled.

"Sam, stop fidgeting," Matt said. "It's bothering me."

"I can't get comfortable."

She heard him shift his body over the ground. She glanced over her shoulder. He'd risen up on his elbow, studying her with such intensity that she feared he could look into her thoughts.

"You've never slept on the ground before?" he asked.

She turned to face him. "Nope. Never been away from home, either."

"You didn't fight in the war?" he asked.

She shook her head. "Did you?"

"Yeah, I did." He dropped back to the ground, shoved his hands beneath his head, and glared at the sky above.

She swallowed hard, not wanting to pry—but incredibly curious. "How old were you?"

He worked his jaw back and forth in that way he had that made her think he was annoyed.

"Fourteen, when I left at the beginning of the war," he finally ground out, not looking at her.

"That's so young," she whispered. She'd known boys who'd gone at twelve. "Were you scared?"

She could see a muscle in his cheek tighten.

"Go to sleep, Sam."

She remembered how Benjamin never talked about the war. Matt seemed to be of the same inclination.

"There's no shame in being scared," she said quietly.

"I'm not ashamed. I've just got nothing to say on the matter," he said tersely.

She knew she wouldn't rest easy if he was upset with her. He could send her home as easily as Jake could. She wanted to smooth the troubled waters, and since she couldn't very well hug him without causing suspicion, all she could do was talk.

"My older brother fought in the war," she told him.

Again he hesitated as though he really didn't want to

know anything about her or her family. "Did he come home?"

"Yes."

He looked back at her. "I'm glad."

"Me, too." She licked her lips, wondering how much to reveal. Matt didn't want a friendship, but she imagined that months out here without talking to someone would be lonely. "He lost his arm at Shiloh. If it weren't for that, he'd be working on this drive, not me. He just didn't think he could handle the job."

He furrowed his brow. "Might take some effort, a little trial and error, but I think he could do it."

She smiled, grateful to hear her own thoughts repeated. "That's what I tried to tell him, but he was too stubborn to give it any thought."

"It wouldn't work at all if he didn't have the desire to do it," Matt said.

"I feel the same way." She felt a blossoming in her heart toward him, knowing that the friendship he wanted to avoid was slowly developing. She already missed Mary Margaret—but then again, Matt wasn't anything like Mary Margaret.

"Did you ever get wounded?" she asked.

She could sense his hesitation to reveal a weakness before he nodded briskly.

"At Gettysburg. Took a bullet in my hip. I limp a little when I get tired."

"You must have been scared," she repeated softly.

"Right down to my boot heels." Suddenly he scowled as though just realizing what he'd admitted. "Go to sleep, kid."

He rolled over, presenting her with his broad back. She curled her fingers to stop herself from reaching out to touch him.

Something inside her was unfurling, an emotion she'd never known before. She enjoyed talking to Matt. Simply looking at him brought her pleasure. She liked having him near.

What was happening to her?

She'd told her mother that none of the hands would figure out she was girl. What she hadn't realized was how desperately she'd want Matt to know she wasn't a boy.

"Time."

Matt awoke, even though the voice had been low and calming. Jake insisted that no one in camp touch or shake someone who was asleep. Most of them had been through the war and automatically reached for their guns when they heard loud noises. Some were even in the habit of shooting before they were fully awake.

With the haze of sleep starting to clear, Matt could see Squirrel grinning at him, revealing the two large protruding front teeth that had earned him his nickname.

"Your watch is coming up," Squirrel told him.

Nodding and yawning, Matt leaned toward Sam until

he was close enough not to startle the boy. He considered leaving him to sleep. They'd done too much jawing before they'd gone to sleep. He'd revealed more than he'd intended. How did the kid manage to work his way through Matt's defenses?

He was young, no doubt about that. Yet there was a maturity to him that seemed at odds with his youth. Matt couldn't quite figure it out. The kid noticed things that most cowboys ignored. He seemed to look at the world— and people—more deeply. Trying to see inside them.

No one else had seemed to notice that Matt preferred to be on the fringe of the group.

If he were smart, he would leave the kid behind. But he didn't want another confrontation with Jake. And that meant taking the boy with him. "Sam?" he whispered.

Sam opened his eyes, looking clearly disoriented.

"It's time for us to take our turn guarding the herd," Matt explained.

Grimacing, Sam sat up, drawing the bulky coat around him. It grew cooler at night, and Matt had his own jacket to wear. But he wouldn't wear it as tightly as the kid did. He liked room to maneuver.

"Shake out your boots before you put them on," Matt ordered as he lifted his own boot, turned it upside down, and pounded the bottom and sides.

"Why?" Sam asked, as he opened his mouth in a big, wide yawn.

"Scorpions, snakes, centipedes . . . they like to crawl into a warm boot for the night."

The kid's eyes grew as round as his mouth. "What?"

Matt couldn't hold back a slight grin. "Don't tell me you're afraid of critters."

"Not afraid. I just don't like them." The boy picked up his boot with only his thumb and forefinger as though he feared it might bite him.

The kid was a contradiction: determined one minute, practically a sissy the next. He had to be younger than he claimed . . .

Matt snatched the boot from Sam's grip and gave it a good thumping. He handed it to the kid before picking up the other one and giving it the same treatment. "Grab us both a cup of coffee from the wagon while I get our horses."

He didn't wait to see if Sam followed, but headed to the remuda, where he selected two good night horses. He began to saddle them up, thinking about his conversation with Sam earlier. There was just something about the kid that made Matt talk, that made him yearn for the friendships he'd had before the war. Friendships the war had stolen from him.

Just as Matt finished getting the horses ready, Sam approached and extended the tin cup toward him. He gulped the coffee down. "Thanks."

"How long do we have to watch them?"

"A shift is two hours. You'll know our shift is up when the Big Dipper moves southwest of the North Star."

The kid looked up at the big expanse of sky. "Is that how cowboys tell time?"

"Yep, most of us don't own watches. The Big Dipper's progress around the North Star keeps track of time for us." He decided the more he explained now, the sooner Jake would let him cut Sam loose. He mounted his horse and watched as the boy did the same.

"So what do we do?" Sam asked as they nudged their horses toward the herd.

"We bed them down in three sections. We'll be responsible for watching the northern group. Just walk around the perimeter. Sing a Texas lullaby if they start to get restless."

"You mean sing a song about Texas?" Sam asked.

Matt kept forgetting that the kid's experience was limited to one milk cow. "A Texas lullaby is when cowboys hum a soothing tune without words."

"I like songs with words. I used to sing to Old Bess," Sam said wistfully.

"Who was Old Bess?"

"Our milk cow."

A cow was a cow. The kid definitely cared too much, and that could sure lead to heartache.

As they neared the herd, Matt veered toward the north and Sam followed.

"You mentioned that you haven't ever been away from home. You're likely to get homesick then," Matt said in a low, even voice. The last thing he wanted to do was start a stampede on Sam's first watch.

"We won't be gone that long," Sam said.

Matt shook his head, even though he thought it unlikely that the kid could see the gesture in the faint moonlight. "It's distance more than time that makes you lonesome for home. The farther you travel, the less likely it seems that you'll return home. And even when you finally . . ." his voice trailed off.

"What?" Sam asked.

He couldn't explain to the kid that when he got home, he didn't feel as though he'd truly returned. "I don't know why it is that when you're around, my tongue starts frolicking. I don't usually talk this much."

"We might end up being friends after all," Sam said, and Matt would have sworn he heard a wistful note in Sam's voice.

"It'll be better if we don't."

"Why?" Sam asked.

"Because I've been charged with being your teacher, not your friend."

"Never did like school much," Sam retorted in a petulant voice.

Matt didn't know any boy who enjoyed sitting in the schoolroom. As a matter of fact, many of the men in the outfit couldn't read or write. Fortunately, he wasn't one of them. He'd finished his schooling at fourteen. His father had insisted he finish before he'd sign the papers giving his permission for Matt to enlist. But Matt always thought he'd gained his real education after that.

"Matt, you promised to tell me how the ranch got its name," the kid reminded him.

He'd hoped Sam would have forgotten his promise, but he should have known better. The kid was as tenacious as a starving dog gnawing on a bone.

What could it hurt to tell the story?

"Well, legend has it that the original owner's wife grew so lonely living on the ranch that her heart broke. She moved back east. And her leaving made the owner's heart break."

"Why didn't he go after her?" Sam asked.

"Said he loved her too much to see her unhappy, but his heart was never the same after that."

"I don't much like that story," Sam said.

Matt didn't either. Like Sam, Matt never had understood why his grandfather hadn't hightailed after his grandmother and convinced her to return to Texas with him. He'd also never understood why she'd left her son behind.

"Matt, is it all right if I sing a song to the cows that has words?" Sam asked.

"Sure, kid. Just keep it low and soothing. We don't

want to make the cows skittish."

The words to "Amazing Grace" began to float on the breeze. Sam had a nice voice, a youthful sound that reminded him of so many drummer boys, singing at night, searching for the courage to march into battle the next day.

But there was an innocence to Sam's singing that was like a balm to Matt's aching heart. Touched him. Made him glad that he'd offered his help to the boy.

He knew Jake was watching him closely. Jake had ordered him to ride drag so he could make a point: on this drive at least, Matt was no better than any of the trail hands. He was to follow orders or he'd be sent packing.

Matt was grateful that Sam seemed to be a hard worker. Together maybe they could ease their way back into Jake's good graces.

Matt didn't much like admitting that Sam's singing touched him as much as it seemed to calm the cows. Sam's eagerness to learn and please reminded Matt too much of himself at a much younger age.

He was glad Sam hadn't gone off to war. Sometimes he wished he hadn't, either.

The hours passed slowly and uneventfully. Eventually, in the distance, Matt saw the riders approaching—the next group who would keep an eye on the slumbering herd.

"All right, kid," he said quietly. "Time for us to head back in."

In the moonlight, he could see the kid's tired smile.

"Don't think I'll have any trouble going to sleep this time," Sam murmured.

Matt knew he couldn't make the same claim. He hadn't had an easy sleep since he'd left for the war.

CHAPTER NINE

The clanging of iron against iron brought Sam awake with a jolt. Every muscle and bone in her body ached; her head throbbed. Her swollen eyes felt gritty. Although she'd slept hard, she hadn't slept long enough to dream.

She squinted through the darkness. The sun wasn't even up yet. Why did she have to be?

Rolling over, she crushed her hat against her face.

"Come on, kid," Matt urged.

"Go away," she grumbled.

He leaned near and she could feel his breath skimming along the nape of her neck, sending delicious shivers skittering down her spine. Why was her body reacting to his nearness in these strange ways?

Nothing like this constant awareness had ever happened to her before. It was almost as frightening as being on this cattle drive, moving farther and farther away from home, away from the familiar.

Because where Matt was concerned, her thoughts and feelings were definitely not familiar.

"If you don't get up, the other fellas are likely to haul

you to the river and toss you in," he warned.

She sat up so fast that she bumped him with her shoulder.

"Ow!" He rubbed his nose.

"I'm sorry."

"That's all right. You really are afraid of the water, aren't you?"

Even in the shadows before dawn, she saw the concern clearly reflected in his eyes. She regretted that she couldn't be completely honest with him. "I'll be all right when crossing a river. I promise."

He nodded briskly, although he didn't look as though he believed her. "If you say so. Stow your bedroll in the back of the supply wagon, get yourself some grub, and join me with the others at the fire."

She noticed then that his bedroll was gone. Had he already been moving about the camp? How did cowboys do this day after day? She supposed once her body adjusted to the routine, she'd do fine.

Right this instant, though, she craved a hot bath and a soft bed, neither of which was available. Just as Matt had taught her, she cautiously checked her boots before pulling them on. Then she rolled up what passed as a bed and carried it to the wagon. She was embarrassed to note that she was the last one sleeping. She didn't want Jake to think she was a slacker, didn't want to give him any reason to replace her at the next town.

Cookie extended a tin plate of johnnycakes toward her. "Eat up," he ordered brusquely.

She wondered if he ever cracked a smile. She grabbed a couple of the johnnycakes and a tin cup of coffee before sauntering to the fire and dropping to the ground beside Matt.

The twins were there, as well as the two fellas she'd caught a quick glimpse of at the river: Slim and Squirrel. Their names suited them. Slim was so skinny that he looked as though he'd have to run around in the rain in order to get wet. Even when he wasn't smiling, Squirrel's teeth hung outside his mouth. She thought it made him look adorable, cute and cuddly—although she doubted he'd want to know she thought of him in that way.

The others seemed incredibly different from Matt. Matt, who appeared older and wiser beyond his years. Matt, who had lines spreading out from the corners of his eyes. She wished she didn't enjoy looking at him so much. None of the young men sitting around the fire were looking at each other. She might give herself away if she kept staring at him.

She needed to mimic these boys. They all appeared to be strangers, and yet they were riding herd together, working to achieve a common goal.

"Why is everyone so quiet?" Sam asked Matt in a low voice.

"Got nothing to say," Slim supplied before Matt could speak.

Sam nodded as though that made sense.

Matt grinned slightly, and her heart did an unusual butterfly flutter.

"Most cowboys don't go to prying," he said. "They figure if a fella wants you to know something, he'll tell you."

"That's the gol' darned truth," Jed said. Or was it Jeb? Sitting beside him, his brother bobbed his head enthusiastically.

She wondered if part of Matt's irritation with her yesterday might have come from her constant prying. But if she didn't question things, how was she going to learn all she needed to know?

"Has everyone been on a cattle drive before?" Sam asked.

"Here and there," Squirrel answered. "Weren't many during the war, but Boss says that they're clamoring for beef up north. Bodes well for those of us with experience. Means there will be another drive next year and the one after that."

Sam's breath hitched as Jake Vaughn crouched beside her. Speak of the devil.

"You fellas gonna jaw all day?" he asked.

"Nah, sir," they all responded while jumping to their feet as though he'd just lit a match and ignited a fire beneath their butts.

Sam started to rise, but Matt wrapped his fingers around her arm. Why did her body want to lean into his? Why did she have to notice how firm and reassuring his hold was? She imagined he had the ability to console a woman when she was feeling down, increase her joy when she was feeling happy.

"Since he squatted beside you, Jake probably wants to talk to you. He just wanted to run the others off first. Right, Jake?"

"That's right."

Sam's breath began to back up into her lungs. The man cut an imposing figure as he studied her.

"How'd you like riding drag?" he asked.

"Liked it just fine." A small lie. She thought she could plant seeds in the dirt covering her face.

"Good, since you'll be doing it again today." He unfolded his body.

"How do you think Sam did?" Matt asked.

Sam wished the ground would crack open and swallow her whole. Why couldn't Matt have left well enough alone?

A corner of Jake's mouth quirked up, and Sam realized that he wasn't nearly as old as she'd thought.

"I thought he did pretty well, for a greenhorn." He turned to go.

"Mr. Vaughn?" Sam asked.

He stopped and stared at her. "Boss."

She nodded quickly. "Right. Boss. Since I did pretty well, I don't see any reason that Matt has to stay by my side. I mean, he could go back to riding point." Anything to get him away from her so she'd stop having these unsettling thoughts about him.

Jake nodded slowly. "Yeah, he could."

Relief rushed through her.

"If I thought that was best . . . which I don't. Just nudge his shadow aside if it gets in your way." He strode toward the wagon.

"It's not fair, his punishing you for being kind and taking me on." Sam tossed her remaining coffee aside and got to her feet.

"All we have to do is teach you everything you need to learn."

"Everything?"

"Everything."

"How long do you think that'll take?"

"You're a pretty fast learner," he said.

Hope spiraled within her. A day more, maybe two and she'd be on her own.

"I reckon two or three years."

"Years?" she repeated.

He tugged his hat down so the brim cast a shadow over his face. "Yeah. Afraid so."

The days rolled along, one following the other. Monotonous days filled with nothing but the boring backsides of cattle and a routine which seldom changed.

As Sam rode beside Matt searching for strays, she couldn't say riding herd was easy. Her body ached and she was more tired than she thought it was possible to be and still be awake. She'd caught Matt sleeping in his saddle as he trailed the herd. She couldn't fathom why he didn't fall from his horse.

Had to be experience. Experience she didn't have that he did. He'd spent much of his time on horses, while she'd spent most of hers in fields.

He'd developed a trust between himself and his horse. A trust he didn't extend to her. It infuriated her that he was so tight lipped and seldom revealed anything about himself. She almost envied the horse.

She wished Mary Margaret was here because she desperately wanted to talk with her about these feelings regarding Matt that she was having. When he was near, she couldn't take her eyes off him. When he wasn't, she thought about him constantly. And when she slept, she dreamed about him.

She couldn't quite put her finger on what the emotions were about. She liked him, she definitely liked him . . . when she wasn't worried that he might figure out she was a girl. He wasn't just watching out for her. He seemed to reluctantly watch out for everyone.

Neither Slim nor Squirrel could write. They would recite their letters home, and Matt would scribble them down for them.

One fella owed Matt for a pair of britches. He'd gone to squat by the fire and a resounding tear had echoed around him. Matt had an extra pair he'd given the fella.

In addition to his bandanna, Matt had given her a pair of gloves. And the little notebook where she could keep her own tally of things owed to others, and things owed to her. So far, no one owed her anything. But she was becoming increasingly indebted to Matt.

He taught her how to guide an errant cow back to the herd without spooking it. How to search for strays, as they were doing now. It seemed no matter how diligently the men watched the cattle at night, one or two always wandered off.

Jake counted the number of cattle every morning and every night. The man was obsessed about not letting down the rancher who had hired him. Sam supposed she couldn't blame him for his diligence.

After all, she was determined not to disappoint Matt.

Even to herself, she had to admit that she was learning a lot faster than she'd expected to. And she thought she was danged good at riding herd.

"There's one," she said pointing toward a thicket.

"You've got good eyes, kid."

She glanced over at him. He was studying her as he tended to do, with one wrist draped over the saddle horn and his hat pushed up slightly off his brow.

"We could have used you when we were rounding the cattle up down south," he said.

"Were you at the ranch?"

"Yep. It's situated between San Antonio and Austin."

She'd seen a map of Texas on the wall at school, so she had a good idea of the state's layout.

"You traveled quite a distance before hiring more hands," she said.

"A lot of the hands are new. Jake decided it would be better to have extra hands on this drive 'cause it's been a while since most of them have herded cattle."

"But no one else has to dog your heels," she pointed out.

He flashed her a grin, the first true smile she'd ever seen on his face. It made her heady, made her feel as though something was waltzing inside her chest.

"You're the only one I had the gall to hire," he said.

"Do you wish you hadn't?"

Matt settled his hat back into place until it caused

shadows to fall across his face. "Nope. You're turning into a first-rate cowhand."

He unhooked his rope from the saddle. "Let's get this cow."

CHAPTER TEN

Sitting near the fire, Sam watched as Squirrel, Slim, Jed, and Jeb played a hand of poker. They hadn't asked her to join them, and she had too much pride to ask.

Matt had gone to talk with Jake, who was off inspecting the herd.

Two weeks had passed, and her confidence in her ability to appear to be a boy was growing stronger. She was talking to the men more, not keeping her distance as much.

She knew that she should remain wary, but she was incredibly lonesome.

Getting Matt to carry on a conversation was like pulling teeth. The rare smiles he'd bestowed upon her haunted her. She imagined he could catch the fancy of any girl he wanted with that devastatingly beautiful smile.

She wanted more smiles from him. More trust.

And she knew that was dangerous. Because if she became close to him—to anyone—she risked the discovery of her secret.

And yet, she was growing so tired of always hovering on the fringes of the camp, watching as friendships between the others began to strengthen, and knowing none of those friendships included her.

She shifted her backside over the log she was sitting on. Jeb glanced up. Even though it was night, they were all still wearing their hats.

"Maybe we ought to invite Sam to join us," he said to no one in particular.

"Only real trail hands can play," Slim said.

"I am a real trail hand," Sam blurted out, irritated that they'd think otherwise.

Squirrel glanced at Slim before shrugging. "Sam's close enough to being a trail hand."

"Not close enough, as far as I'm concerned," Slim said. "I haven't seen Sam catch a snipe yet."

"What's a snipe?" Sam asked, without thinking.

All four trail hands looked at her as though she were crazy.

"Surely you know what a snipe is," Jed said.

"All cowboys know what a snipe is," Jeb said.

"Think, Sam," Squirrel prodded, "deep down inside, you know what a snipe is, don't you?"

"It's something every real cowboy knows without being told," Slim added.

Sam swallowed hard. She wanted to measure up something fierce. She nodded. "Yeah, yeah, I know what a snipe is. I just wasn't thinking."

"Well, to truly belong, you have to catch one. It's a rite

of passage. We all did it before you signed up," Slim said.

The others grinned broadly and nodded.

"So what do I do?" Sam asked.

"Go tell Cookie you're going snipe hunting. He'll give you a burlap sack." Slim stood. "I'll get our horses and take you to where I spotted a snipe hole earlier."

"Maybe I should wait for Matt," Sam said hesitantly.

"Snipes are shy," Slim explained. "They don't come out if there's more than one person around. Snipe hunting is a solitary endeavor."

"'Sides, Matt wouldn't take you snipe hunting. He's afraid of snipes," Squirrel said.

"Iffen you want to be considered a real trail hand, you've gotta do this," Slim said. "I can get you out there and back before Matt returns."

Sam contemplated facing Matt's anger. He'd told her to stay here, but she needed to show him and Jake that she could take care of herself. She nodded before she lost her courage. "All right, I'll do it."

She tromped over to the wagon where Cookie was washing up his pots and pans. "Cookie, could I borrow a burlap sack?"

"What fer?" he asked grumpily.

"I'm going to hunt for a snipe."

His bushy white eyebrows shot up to his balding pate. "Them fellas over there put you up to this?"

She nodded.

He shook his head. "Can't believe it took 'em this long. They send most greenhorns out on their first night."

"Don't suppose you'd like to tell me what a snipe looks like?" she asked.

"Oh, you'll know it when you see it," Cookie assured her. He cackled like an old woman. "You'll know it when you dadgum see it."

Matt noticed it the instant he walked into the camp. Expectancy hung heavy in the air. He didn't like it. Didn't like it one bit.

He glanced around. Sam was nowhere to be seen. Trepidation sliced through him. He strode to the fire where the troublesome foursome were busy playing cards.

"Where's Sam?" he demanded.

Squirrel guffawed while the rest of them snickered.

"Where is he?" Matt insisted.

"Sent him snipe hunting," Slim said, grinning like a carved pumpkin at Halloween.

Matt should have known. The single most popular cowboy prank was to send new trail hands snipe hunting. Just take them out to the middle of nowhere and tell them to bag a snipe. He'd never understood why cowboys thought it was funny to send someone on a wild-goose chase after an imaginary critter.

He should have thought to warn the kid, but he'd been more concerned with keeping his distance emotionally when he couldn't do it physically. He'd been teaching the kid how to be a first-rate trail hand. He just hadn't given any thought to teaching him how to be a cowboy.

"Why did you have to go and do that? He's just a kid," Matt said.

"Ain't no harm in it," Jed said. "It's part of being a cowboy."

"Where did you take him?" Matt asked.

Slim jerked his head to the side. "Far enough away from the cattle that he wouldn't start a stampede."

"Come on, Matt. Don't look so mad," Jed said. "We was just having some fun with the kid."

"But that kid is my responsibility. He's never been away from home." He looked into the darkness. Trees lined the river, but once he moved beyond the trees, there was nothing but emptiness and the cattle that were bedded down for the night.

"You idiots," he muttered as he headed for the remuda to re-saddle his horse.

"Ah, Matt, the kid will be all right," someone called after him.

But what if he wasn't? His heart was hammering. What if he wasn't?

It took Sam all of fifteen minutes to figure out she'd been duped.

She'd had her suspicions when Slim hadn't been able to

remember exactly where he'd seen the snipe hole, but he'd been sure she'd find it if he left her here alone.

In the moonlight, she'd seen an armadillo scurry across the land. She heard the lowing of the distant cattle.

She'd never heard of a snipe, and the more she thought about the sly glances the fellas had been passing among themselves while discussing snipe hunting, the more she'd realized she was on the wrong end of a prank.

She should have been furious—hurt, even. But she had a feeling that snipe hunting was exactly what Slim had indicated it was—a rite of passage. She wouldn't have minded the prank so much if it wasn't dark and she wasn't alone.

She had a gun that she'd never fired. A horse she'd never ridden except to this spot. And an empty burlap sack.

And when she returned to camp, she'd no doubt discover Matt's anger. Or his disappointment that she'd been foolish enough to believe the boys.

She saw a silhouette emerging from the darkness and immediately recognized the man by the way he sat in the saddle and the shape of his shoulders. She was unsettled by how well she knew even his outline.

He drew his horse to a halt in front of her, and she heard his sigh of annoyance.

"Kid, what were you thinking to let them leave you out here alone?" he scolded.

She felt the tears sting her eyes. Of all the things she'd

feared when she'd decided to disguise herself as a boy, being without a friend hadn't been one of them.

But boys didn't cry, so she had to shore up her emotions, and the quickest way was with anger. "Will you stop calling me 'kid'? My name is Sam."

"I know your name," he mumbled.

"Then use it," she spat out. "Unless you're afraid."

"Why would I be afraid?"

"Using my name might make us seem like friends. Calling me 'kid' helps you keep this distance between us that you're so all-fired anxious to keep."

"Look, kid, I told you we weren't going to be friends."

"Did you tell everyone else that they couldn't be friends with me, either?"

"Of course not," he said. "Is that the reason you let them talk you into coming out here? So you could be friends with them?"

"What if it is?"

"Then it was a pretty stupid reason."

More tears surfaced. He was right—she'd been gullible. She quickly turned away so he wouldn't see the moonlight reflecting in her pool of tears.

The saddle creaked as he dismounted.

She felt his nearness even though he wasn't touching her.

"I just wanted to belong. I work so hard, Matt, but I'm so dadgum lonely. I wasn't expecting not to have any friends." With the back of her hand, she swiped roughly at the tears that had rolled onto her cheeks. She couldn't explain the loneliness of being the only girl surrounded by males. Not when she was supposed to be a boy.

"Geez, Sam, don't cry," he said quietly.

"I'm not crying." She lied. So much for keeping her promise to be honest. She stomped away from him, irritated with her weakness, more irritated with him for being strong.

"Sam, you promised no more lies."

She spun on her heel and marched toward him. "All right, then. Here's the truth." She jabbed her finger into his chest, not surprised it felt like hitting it against a brick wall. "I'm hundreds of miles from home, from anyone who cares about me. I could get killed—"

"Don't say that!" he interrupted. "You're not going to die out here."

"I might. And no one would care."

"I'd care."

"No, you wouldn't. Friends care, Matt. You told me we weren't going to be friends. I'm trying, but it's really hard. Not having a single friend, waking up to your scowling face. Going to sleep without even hearing a good-night." She spun away. She sounded like a girl now, and that was the last thing she'd intended. She didn't mind the calluses on her hands, but she was starting to feel them forming on her heart. She didn't want to be as hard as Matt or Jake or Cookie.

"Cowboys don't make good friends, Sam. Most are running from something."

She glanced over her shoulder at him. "What are you running from, Matt?"

He dropped his gaze and began kicking the ground with the toe of his boot. He kept telling her not to lie, but with his silence he was as guilty as she was of not being honest. But she'd never convince him of that.

"I feel like such a fool," she admitted. "Snipe hunting. The others will never respect me, now that I was so stupid," she added.

"You weren't that stupid," he said, lifting his gaze to hers. "Went snipe hunting myself when I was twelve."

"You did?"

"Sure. Every cowboy does. Can't call yourself a real cowboy if you haven't. I imagine even Jake has gone snipe hunting."

"Then why were you so mad at me?"

"I feel responsible for you, Sam, and I'm afraid I'm going to let you down. Sounds as though that's exactly what I'm doing. I'll try to be a tad more friendly."

He said "friendly" as though it was something he was afraid of stepping in and having to scrape off the bottom of his boot. She wanted to tell him not to do her any more favors, but the truth was, of all the men on the cattle drive, Matt was the one she most wanted to be friends with.

"It would help if Jake wouldn't watch us so closely," she said.

"I agree. As a matter of fact, that's what I went to talk to him about. But he's not comfortable with me cutting you loose yet, so I guess we're stuck with each other." He mounted his horse. "Come on. Let's head back and I'll teach you how to get even playing poker with those boys."

CHAPTER ELEVEN

A few days later, Matt sat beneath a tree while Sam held a small mirror in front of him. Matt carefully scraped the bristly beard off his chin. He'd started growing whiskers when he was fifteen. The last year or so, they'd actually started to thicken. Sam didn't even have peach fuzz yet. He wondered if the boy was as eager to have hair on his face as Matt had been.

"What do you think, Sam? Think I got enough here for a decent mustache?" Sucking his upper lip into his mouth, he studied the growth above his lip. He was actually beginning to enjoy being friends with Sam. The kid hung onto every word Matt said as though he'd invented it.

He lifted his gaze above his reflection and watched as twin spots of color appeared on Sam's cheeks. Until he'd met Sam, Matt wasn't sure that he'd ever seen a fella blush.

"What do you think?" he asked again. "Honestly now. No matter what you say, it won't hurt my feelings."

"I think you look better without the mustache."

Matt angled his face and returned his gaze to the mirror. "I think you're right."

He stretched his upper lip taut and brushed some

lathered soap over it. With the straight razor, he scraped away the remaining whiskers. Wouldn't do to have any nicks tonight.

When he was finished, he looked with satisfaction at his reflection. He combed his fingers through his hair. "You did a fine job trimming my hair. Sure you don't want me to cut yours?"

"I'm sure," Sam said hastily.

Grinning, Matt reached into his bag of supplies. He poured some Bay Rum cologne into his palm before patting it over his cheeks and chin. "Want some?" he asked Sam.

Sam shook his head. The boy actually looked frightened.

"Sam, everything will be all right tonight," he assured him.

"I really don't want to go, Matt."

Matt leaned forward and planted his elbows on his thighs. "Look, Sam, it's not every day that we run across a town that invites us to a barn dance. Another week or so and we're going to be at the Red River. No towns on the other side for miles and miles. A cowboy has to take his fun where he can."

"But I feel bad about going."

"Jake put everyone's name in a hat," he reminded Sam. "He drew out the six who have to stay behind and herd cattle."

"It doesn't seem fair."

"But that's the way it's always done. The cattle come first. A cowboy knows that when he signs up. We can't leave the cows on their own. Somebody has to watch them. Drawing names out of a hat in order to determine who stays behind is the best way," he explained patiently.

He'd already explained it once when Jake had first come into camp and announced that they had the invite. Matt couldn't understand why Sam was so opposed to going out and having a good time, especially when there were bound to be a few gals in attendance. Matt might prefer not to be friends with the men he worked with, but he had no qualms at all about becoming friends with a young lady or two.

"But I don't want to go," Sam insisted.

"If you stay behind, one of those six men will want to go to the dance in your place. We'd have to have another drawing. I don't think that would sit well with Jake."

In truth, he didn't think Jake would care. His only fear was that if Sam didn't go, Matt would be ordered to stay behind. He was in the mood for some dancing, and he wanted Sam to have some fun. The boy didn't seem to know much about fun. He never took a dip in the river, since he couldn't swim. He seldom played cards, because he didn't like the thought of losing any hard-earned money. He never played pranks on the other cowboys. As far as Matt could see, he was as serious as they came.

But the boy had dreams—dreams of all the things he could purchase with the money he'd earn at the end of the drive. And Matt certainly couldn't complain about how quickly the kid learned a new task. He wasn't sure if he'd ever known a fella to catch on to herding cattle with the ability that Sam did.

"Come on, Sam. Jake took two cows over to them earlier so we'll have lots of beef to eat tonight. Some farmer's wife is bound to bake an apple pie or two. You can't turn away from the chance to eat a slice of fresh apple pie. Besides, there's probably going to be several farmers' daughters in attendance. Cookie is taking his fiddle, so we'll have music and dancing. It'll be fun."

But Sam took to studying his gloves as though he'd never seen them before. Matt had given him the gloves, and they'd practically swallowed Sam's small hands. How did a boy get such dainty-looking hands? Matt figured they were an embarrassment to him. Sam had quickly borrowed needle and thread from Cookie and taken in the seams so the gloves fit better. He wondered if Sam was even fourteen yet. He sure had a hard time believing he was anywhere close to being sixteen.

"I don't know any of these people," Sam muttered.

"You know me. Slim, Squirrel, Jeb." Poor Jed. His name had been pulled out of the hat. Matt had a feeling that Jake had rigged the drawing so one of the twins would have to stay behind. The last night of round-up, the boys had a wild time pretending to be each other. "Come on, Sam, this might be our last chance to have some fun for a while."

Sam hesitated, and Matt decided to play his final card. With a deep sigh, he sat back against the tree. "All right. You win. We won't go."

Sam's eyes widened. "What do you mean *we?* You can go without me."

"Nah, I can't. Jake said you have to stay as close to me as my shadow. So I figure if you don't want to go, then I need to stay behind as well so you can obey his order." He felt a twinge of guilt when he saw the disappointment cross Sam's face. He couldn't understand Sam's reluctance to go, but he was fairly certain if he could just get Sam to the dance, he'd enjoy himself.

"Oh, all right. I'll go," Sam said petulantly.

"You'll be glad, Sam. I promise you're gonna have the best time of your life."

Sam was having the worst time of her life.

Standing within the shadows of a corner in the barn, she watched all the goings-on, trying to memorize the various aspects of the night so she could share them with Mary Margaret.

The beef, beans, and pies had tasted delicious. They'd reminded her of home and made her a trifle homesick.

The fiddle players struck up a lively tune as soon as

they finished a slower melody. Fast. Slow. Fast. Slow. As much as she tried to prevent it, her foot tapped to the beat of the music.

The people were friendly. The young ladies, much to her annoyance, were especially so.

For someone who had claimed that he didn't want to make friends, Matt sure wasn't heeding his own advice tonight. He was getting to be best friends with several of the ladies. He also seemed to be one smooth dancer.

From the moment that the music had started, he hadn't missed a single dance. Girls were batting their eyelashes at him and smiling with their lips pulled back so far that Sam wondered if they wanted to make sure he knew they possessed all their teeth.

She didn't mean to have unkind thoughts. It was just that watching all that flirting made her downright miserable. Dressed in her boy's clothing, Sam had never felt so dowdy or longed so intensely for a dress.

She hated herself for envying the girls' dresses and their long hair. Hair that flowed down their backs or was swept on top of their heads. She loathed seeing the way that Matt smiled at all the girls, as though each one was special.

His blue eyes held a magical warmth, a warmth he'd never bestowed upon her. But why would he? In his eyes, she was a boy. He had no idea that he'd begun to wander through her dreams.

The music stopped and she watched as he walked his most recent partner to the table and ladled some lemonade into a glass for her. The girl gave him a flirtatious smile. Matt flashed her a returning grin as though they were sharing something special. Sam hated watching, but she couldn't make herself look away.

What she wouldn't give for Matt to look at her like that.

"Hey, Sam," Squirrel said as he joined her and leaned against a beam. "How come you ain't dancin'?"

Since her snipe-hunting expedition, the other hands had been more accepting of her. She supposed it was as they'd told her—a rite of passage. Something she'd needed to do in order to belong.

"Don't want to dance." Which wasn't exactly true. She did want to dance—but she wanted to dance with Matt, and the only way that would happen would be if she revealed her secret. Her experience as a trail hand would come to an abrupt halt here and now if she did that.

"Cookie can sure make that fiddle talk, can't he?" Squirrel asked.

"Yep."

"I like the fast dances myself. Think Matt likes the slow ones."

"Appears so," she said curtly.

The next tune started up. She saw the girl set her glass aside. Matt took her hand and led her back to the dance area. Sam didn't know why she had to feel so sad. Matt was having a good time. She should be happy for him.

"The girls surely do seem to favor Matt," Squirrel said.

They surely did. She heaved a sigh. "How long do you think we're staying here?"

"'Till Boss says it's time to go. Some widow has taken a fancy to him, though, so it might be a while."

She wondered if she could find her way back to the herd by herself. There were no landmarks to speak of and she was unfamiliar with the area. She didn't want to risk getting lost and losing her chance to get that money.

"I'm gonna go get something else to eat. Wanna come?" he asked.

She shook her head. "Nope. But thanks, Squirrel." She angled her head thoughtfully. "What's your real name, anyway?"

"You'll laugh."

She grinned. "No, I won't."

"Rupert." He shook his head. "Don't know what my ma was thinking."

"She was probably thinking that she loved you."

He grinned. "Reckon. Sure you don't want to come and eat? In one of the stalls, folks is bobbin' for apples. Thought I might give that a go."

She patted her stomach. "I'm full, but thanks for the invite."

He wandered away. She slipped farther into the

shadowed corner and searched the dance area until she spotted Matt again.

Incredibly handsome, he held the girl as though she was a precious gift.

Listening closely, Sam allowed more than the music to seep inside her. She allowed her imagination in, giving it free rein.

She imagined she was that girl, encircled by Matt's strong arms. The flames from the lanterns flickered around her and Matt.

She was no longer dressed in britches. She was wearing a new dress, sewn from blue calico. She wasn't wearing boots. She was wearing black shoes buttoned up to her calf. And her hair wasn't curling over the top of her head. It was cascading down her back to her waist, brushed to a glistening sheen.

And Matt.

He was looking at her as though she were the only girl in the barn with whom he wanted to waltz. Their steps began to slow. In her mind, he drew her closer and lowered his mouth to hers . . .

The music stopped playing, and she snapped out of her reverie. With disappointment reeling through her, she watched as he walked out of the barn with his arm around the girl. She didn't want to think about what they might be doing outside.

Or how badly she wanted him to be doing it with her.

For pity's sake! What was wrong with her?

Several minutes later she saw Matt come back into the barn. The girl sashayed away from him. His hair looked as though she'd repeatedly combed her fingers through it. It hurt Sam too much to think about it.

Matt began searching the barn. Suddenly his eyes lit upon her and he strode toward her.

Her heart began pounding and her palms grew damp. He looked so incredibly handsome tonight with his clean-shaven face, his washed and neatly trimmed hair. She had done a good job cutting his hair so she knew exactly what it had felt like when that brazen hussy had run her fingers through it outside.

Like all the men, he'd bathed in the river and brought out a fresh set of clothes.

"Why are you hiding over here, Sam?" he asked.

Because she was terrified that she might do or say something that would give her away. "I'm just not comfortable here, Matt. I really want to go back to the herd."

He shook his head. "I don't understand. Everyone is so nice."

"Especially the girls, right?" She wished she'd bitten off her tongue before she'd said that.

He grinned broadly. "Yeah, they are. You should give talking to one of them a try."

"So I can make a fool out of myself like you're doing?

You're going to wear out the soles of your boots with all that dancin'."

"Sam, I don't understand what's bothering you."

She didn't either. She only knew that she didn't like seeing him talking to, smiling at, or dancing with other girls. "Nothing is bothering me that can't be fixed by leaving."

Matt leaned close, and his Bay Rum scent wafted around her. "There are a couple here who are real free with their kisses. You ought to take a short walk with one of them."

"No, thanks. When I kiss someone, it's gonna be because that someone is special." She brushed past him. She didn't want to hear about all the kisses he was bestowing upon the girls here but would never bestow upon her.

She headed out of the barn, into the night. Matt probably thought she was loco, but she hadn't wanted to come here anyway. Her first dance . . . her very first dance, and she was here pretending she was a boy. She was watching the young men dance with the girls, flirt with them, talk with them.

She had never experienced any of those exciting, exhilarating things. She wasn't only jealous of Matt, she was jealous of every girl who hadn't had to cut her hair or put on her brother's old clothes.

She came to a stop beside the corral and gave herself a

mental shake. No one had forced her to chop off her hair. She'd wanted to do it. And wearing Nate's clothes wasn't that bad. They afforded her more freedom. She actually liked them when she wasn't at a dance.

She stepped onto the first railing of the fence and folded her arms across the top. All their horses were stirring about inside the enclosure. Hopefully Jake would call an end to all the fun and they would head back to camp soon.

"Sam?"

She squeezed her eyes shut at the sound of Matt's concerned voice. "Matt, just ignore me. I don't know what's wrong with me tonight."

Opening her eyes, she turned her face toward him. Standing on the rung, she found herself at eye-level with him. "Go back in and have some fun."

"I can't do that, Sam. Not when you're having such a miserable time."

"Matt, for tonight, just forget Jake's orders. Forget I'm your responsibility," she told him.

"I might forget all that, Sam, but I can't forget that you're becoming my friend. And I've figured out what's bothering you," he said.

"Matt, you can't know," she said honestly.

"But I do. You've never courted a girl, have you?" he asked quietly.

She turned her attention back to the horses. "Matt—"

"Have you?" he insisted.

"No." That much, at least, was the truth.

"I remember how nervous I was the first time I danced with a girl. You just have to realize that you're doing the girl a favor by dancing with her."

Sam looked at him and narrowed her eyes. "Maybe she's doing you one by dancing with you."

He grinned in the moonlight. "You'll get no argument from me on that. And when it comes to kissing—"

"I'm definitely not ready for kissing," she blurted out.

He chuckled low. "All right, Sam. Just take it slow. If you don't want to dance, just find a girl to talk to."

"Maybe I will," she said, knowing good and well she wouldn't.

"I'm going to head back inside, then, find me a gal to twirl around the floor." He ruffled Sam's hair. "Honestly, Sam, you ought to give dancing a try. Girls are soft and they smell so good. Once you get to talking to them, it's not that hard to move on to dancing and then kissing."

She watched him walk off, then she leaned against the barn. She didn't want to dance with a girl. For that matter, she didn't want to dance with another fella, either. She just wanted to dance with Matt.

She wrapped her arms around herself in an attempt to

hold all the feelings deep inside her. She was afraid to give them a name, to contemplate them too much.

She was terrified that she was falling in love with him.

And he'd never return that love. He thought Sam was a boy. And if he ever found out that Sam was a girl . . . he wouldn't love her then, either. How could he love someone who had deceived him?

CHAPTER TWELVE

The undulating prairie grasses rolled out before them like a vast expanse of emptiness. As Sam's horse plodded along beside Matt's, she couldn't help but feel overwhelmed by the aching chasm of loneliness that crept over her.

In the days that had passed since the dance, Sam had repeatedly tried to put her emotions back on an even keel. But they wouldn't cooperate. Ever since she'd imagined herself dancing with Matt, she'd realized that she was falling for him hard.

For her, the most innocent of moments was anything but guileless.

She listened to his even breathing at night while they lay side by side. It meant nothing to him, of course. He was simply sleeping beside one of the trail hands.

But sometimes, she would watch him. And wonder how it might have been between them if she'd never cut her hair and taken on the disguise of a boy.

Would she have caught his attention at the dance? Would he have approached her? Taken a few minutes to talk with her? Would he have asked her to dance? Would he have escorted her out of the barn for a passionate kiss?

She thought about the kiss most of all. Would he kiss her slowly, take his time, make her toes curl? Would he whisper in her ear that he loved her?

"Sam?"

Sam jerked out of her reverie at the sound of his voice. Grateful that her bandanna hid her burning cheeks, she glanced over at Matt. "Yeah?"

He nudged his horse closer to hers. "It looked like you were drifting off. You gotta pay attention. The least little thing can start a stampede."

She heaved a sigh and lied. "I *was* paying attention."

"Some girl at the dance catch your fancy?" His eyes were sparkling and she imagined that beneath his bandanna he was grinning.

"No," she replied curtly. "Why would you think that?"

"Because it was right after that dance that you started getting those faraway looks in your eyes. And usually when a fella is gazing at nothing, he's thinking about a woman."

"Did someone at the dance catch your fancy?" she dared to ask.

"There were a couple of girls who I thought were pretty." Now he got a faraway look in his eye. "And a couple who sure were skilled when it came to kissing."

She had a strong need to stomp her foot in frustration, but that was a little hard to do when her feet were in the stirrups. He had no idea that every time he talked about girls he was tormenting her.

A week later Sam was staring at the churning waters of the Red River. She was on the verge of leaving Texas . . . going into Indian Territory and beyond that into Kansas and Missouri.

If she had any doubts about going forward, she knew she needed to address them now. Once she crossed the Red, she'd have no opportunity to go back—at least, not alone. But as much as she could smell the muddy river, she could smell the scent of money more.

Just a few more weeks and she would have completed the journey. She'd be heading home, and she'd never see Matt again. Excitement at the prospect of being with her family dimmed when she thought of leaving Matt.

She'd miss him. They'd formed a tentative friendship, a bond that she knew would snap in two if he ever discovered the truth about her.

The cattle had been crossing the river for much of the day. They seemed to be proud of their swimming skills. Their bodies sank below the surface of the river. All she could see were their heads and their horns. So many cattle swimming across.

And as usual, she and Matt were near the tail end of the herd.

"If you want, we can wait until all the cattle are on the other side before we swim our horses across," Matt said as he sat on his horse beside hers.

Neither of them wore their bandannas pulled up over their faces. The cattle weren't kicking up dust. They were stirring up the water.

"I'm not afraid of the water. Besides, isn't a trail hand supposed to go across with the cattle?" she asked.

"Yeah, but—"

She sliced her gaze over to him, daring him to say she needed special treatment simply because she was his responsibility.

"Just remember to keep a strong grip on your saddle horn," he said. "A tight hold on the reins. The saddle will get slippery, but you'll be all right as long as you keep your seat."

She wished she could ease his worry by confessing that she knew how to swim, but then she'd have to explain why she hadn't ever taken a dip in the rivers they'd traveled along or camped near. They hadn't had to cross the others because they'd run north and south. But this one ran west to east.

"I'll be fine, Matt."

"Stay close to me, Sam," he ordered before kicking his

horse and urging it down the embankment.

Stay close to him. She'd been riding the trail for six weeks. She knew her way around the cattle. He thought she was a kid who needed protecting. It irritated her no end.

She knew his caring shouldn't, but it did.

Cinnamon balked at the water's edge. The water was swirling from all the cattle milling around. She nudged the mare's flanks. "Come on, girl, we gotta get."

Her horse headed into the water, but by now several cows had separated Sam from Matt. She wasn't worried, though. She was confident she could handle her horse.

The water began to lap at her calves. Then it rose to her thighs. The force of the current surprised her. It hadn't looked that strong from the bank.

The cattle bawled. It seemed that some wanted to turn back to the shore from which they'd come. Others were moving in closer, their horns clacking and becoming entangled.

A cow shoved up against her. Cinnamon whinnied. The steer turned its head, its huge horns making a wide arc. Sam jerked back and balanced precariously on the slippery saddle.

With her arms flailing, she lost her seating and splashed into the water. She went beneath the murky depths. Something bumped into her from one side, something else from the other. Furry, warm. Cows. It had to be cows.

She fought her way to the surface and gasped for air. Surrounded by huge beasts, she was being knocked about. She couldn't see Cinnamon.

The water started to drag her down. She went back under. While she struggled and kicked against the current, she worked her coat off. With it gone, she found it easier to stroke, to claw her way to the top.

She broke through to the surface, took a gulp of precious air, and immediately found herself pulled back under by the strong current and the undertow created by the milling cattle.

Something hard kicked her in the side, and white lightning exploded before her closed eyes. She had to get free. Had to get free.

But everywhere she turned, she found herself hemmed in by bellies, legs, and rumps.

There was no escape.

"Sam!" Matt yelled.

His gut tightened into a painful knot as he watched Sam come up for air before slipping beneath the murky, reddish-brown water of the river. Woven tightly together, the cattle were bawling.

Standing in the stirrups, Matt swung his leg clear of the saddle before leaping onto the back of a steer. Horns clacked around him as he scrambled onto the shoulders of another longhorn—all the while straining to keep Sam within his sight. He could see Sam thrashing through the water, trying desperately to paddle.

He jumped to the next steer. He saw Sam come back up, the drenched clothing had to be weighing the boy down.

The beast Matt was on started to roll. He scrambled across to the next one, and then he spotted a hole between the animals. Taking a deep breath, he dived into it.

Working his way past bellies and legs, he swam to where he hoped he'd find Sam. He broke through the surface of the water, breathing harshly. He saw Sam's flailing arms.

With sure strokes born of desperation, he swam toward the kid. He fought the rapid current, ducked to avoid a razor-sharp horn. He was not going to let the boy drown. No way, no how. He wasn't going to lose Sam the way he'd lost so many friends during the war.

As he neared, Sam went under. Reaching out, clawing through the water, he grabbed Sam's arm and jerked him up. White as a sheet, Sam was gasping for breath, the lines around his mouth tight. A sure sign of pain. Had a steer gored him? Matt had known that to happen before.

"It's all right, Sam, I've got you!" He slipped his arm beneath Sam's armpits and began churning through the water as best as he could with only one arm. He headed for the Texas side of the river because it was closer. They could always cross to the other side later, once he knew for certain that Sam was unharmed. He could feel Sam trembling, quivering.

As he neared the bank, the bottom of the river met his boots. Standing, he hauled Sam to his feet. Had he ever noticed how slight Sam was? How thin? The kid hardly weighed anything at all.

The mud sucked at Matt's boots as he dragged Sam to the shore. Gently releasing Sam, he bent over, planted his hands on his thighs, and fought to draw air into his aching lungs. Sam crawled to a tree, sat up slightly, and leaned against it, breathing harshly.

"You were supposed"—he gasped for air—"to stay close by me."

Sam nodded. He was turned away, holding his side.

"Sam?"

"I'm . . . okay."

"A steer probably kicked you. Let me take a look-see at your ribs." He crouched beside the boy. Putting his hand on Sam's shoulder, he turned him slightly.

And froze.

Sam's drenched clothes were plastered to his body, outlining small hills and shallow valleys.

Hills? Valleys?

Several buttons on Sam's shirt had come loose. The material parted to reveal a glistening wet mound of flesh, a gentle swelling where there should have been nothing but flatness.

Matt scrambled back as though Sam had suddenly burst into flames. "Gawd Almighty! You're a girl!"

CHAPTER THIRTEEN

Livid, Matt paced. His boot heels hit the ground with one resounding thud after another. A girl. Sam was a blasted girl!

The entire time while he'd been eating with Sam and sleeping beside him—*her, her*—Sam had been a girl. Matt had ridden beside her during the day and late at night, had taught her to play poker and to rope calves.

He felt like such a fool. How could he not have known?

He'd rather face the Union Army than Jake when he found out Matt had hired a female! Matt was responsible for bringing a girl onto this cattle drive!

What would his father say when he found out? He'd wonder if Matt had forgotten to bring his common sense home from the war!

Could anything be more humiliating . . . or infuriating? He'd been duped! Bamboozled. Tricked.

He spun around and glared at Sam.

Only this time—for the very first time—he wasn't looking at Sam the *boy*, the *kid*, he was staring at Sam the *girl*. That face that would never produce whiskers looked delicate, with its tiny, pert nose and soft cheeks. Long lashes framed incredible green eyes. The fact that she suddenly *looked* like a girl angered him even more.

"You lied to us! From the start, you've been lying through your teeth."

It looked as though Sam was quickly agreeing with him. Her head bobbed up and down rapidly. But then he realized Sam was shaking uncontrollably. Dang it!

"Matt!"

He heard Jake's voice and hurried to the water's edge. He saw Jake on the opposite bank. All the cattle had crossed over and were being prodded farther into the Indian Territory. Everyone was on the far side of the river. Everyone except Sam and him.

"What's going on over there?" Jake yelled. "Are you both all right?"

He cupped his hands close to his mouth to be certain he was heard. "We're fine!"

"Need me to come back across?"

That was the very last thing Matt wanted at this moment.

"No. Sam's a little shaken, but I can handle it. We'll catch up in a while!"

He released a sigh of relief when Jake waved his hand in the air to signal he'd heard Matt and was accepting his judgment on the matter. Jake turned his horse around and headed away from the river.

Catch up, my foot, Matt thought. *I'll catch up, but Sam's heading back the way she came.*

As soon as she stopped shivering like someone packed in a tub of ice. He waded into the water and grabbed the reins to his horse. He was fortunate the animal had returned to this shore. He rubbed Robert E. Lee's nose. "Good boy."

He led him back into the thicket where Sam was still huddled. Dang it! Sam's lips were turning blue. Matt removed his saddlebags and saddle. He jerked the blankets off and knelt in front of Sam.

"Here." He draped the damp blankets around Sam's shoulders.

He wished he had dry blankets to offer her, but he'd have to cross the river and hightail it to the wagon. Since it had crossed the river at the front of the herd, it would be miles away. And he couldn't leave Sam alone. As much as he wanted to, he felt an obligation to take care of her until she was out of his sight. Then he'd be able to get her out of his mind.

Sam continued to tremble. His green—no, *her*—green eyes were large and round, but it didn't look as though she was really looking at anything.

"Shock. You're probably in some sort of shock." He'd seen that often enough during the war—after a battle. Whenever a fella couldn't quite figure out if he'd really managed to survive—and if he had, how? "You're all right, Sam, you hear me?"

Sam nodded.

If Sam had been a boy, Matt would have stripped off his soaked clothes. As it was, he tucked one blanket in closer to her body, then wrapped another around her legs. "I'm gonna start a fire."

Swearing softly beneath his breath, cursing his gullibility, he quickly gathered small twigs, some larger fallen branches, and dry driftwood. Then he grabbed his saddlebag and scrounged through it until he found the metal box where he kept his matches housed. During the war he'd learned the value of keeping his matches dry.

After striking a match, he carried the flame to the small pile of leaves and twigs. He could hear Sam's teeth clattering. Matt was mad enough to spit and more worried than he'd ever been in his entire life.

He'd accepted responsibility for Sam the boy . . . he couldn't discharge it just because he'd discovered Sam was a girl. If anything, he felt more responsible now.

And deceived.

The flame caught and the leaves began to crackle as they ignited and spread the fire.

He didn't want to remember all the things he'd shared with Sam the boy. He'd begun lowering his defenses, allowing a friendship to develop with the kid—only the relationship had been false, built on a bald-faced lie.

Matt had always been honest with Sam, and Sam had never been honest with him.

Resting on his haunches, Matt twisted around. A blue shadow was circling her blue lips. The blankets weren't warming her enough and the fire might not take the chill off quickly enough. He unfolded his body and jerked his shirt off. He spread it over a bush close to the fire so it would be dry when he was ready for it.

He walked over to her and crouched beside her. He wanted to chew her up and spit her out. "I'm mad enough to swallow a horned toad backward."

She bobbed her head. "I know. W-w-what are y-y-you going to do?"

"We gotta get you warm. Body heat's the fastest way." Sitting, he worked his back against the tree. He drew her onto his lap, pressing her close against his chest, wrapping his arms tightly around her.

She nestled her head into the crook of his shoulder. "I-I'm s-sorry, Matt," she croaked.

"Not as sorry as you're gonna be," he promised.

Briskly he rubbed his hands up and down her arms, trying to create friction and heat. He heard her teeth tapping together. The water had been cool, but he suspected it was more her harrowing plunge into the river that had her quaking so badly.

He'd never been this furious in his entire life. Or embarrassed by all the private things he'd revealed.

Including his bare backside!

No wonder Sam had run off. Gawd almighty!

"I-I do know how to s-swim," she said, as though she knew the direction his mind was headed.

"Then you were lying when you told me you didn't." His entire body heated up with the memory of shucking his clothes in front of her. If her damp clothes weren't between them, he figured he'd scald her skin with his embarrassment.

She nodded jerkily. "When I . . . f-fell in the r-river . . . the current was too strong, and the cattle kept getting in my way," she stammered.

"Did you lie about everything?" he asked, unable to rein in his anger. It slithered through his voice like a snake about to strike. Yet he took no comfort in her blanching.

"Not my name."

"Your parents named you Sam?" he asked, no longer willing to believe anything she told him.

"Samantha."

He could see her as a Samantha. And for some reason, that image irritated him even more.

"I didn't lie about my age, either."

Then she *was* sixteen. At least now he knew why she didn't have any danged whiskers. Her age had nothing to do with her soft cheeks or her quiet voice.

"Or the reason that I wanted to come on this cattle drive."

She tilted her head back and held his gaze. It was strange how knowing now that she was female made her eyes seem much softer, much greener. Drops of water clung to her spiked eyelashes, and he fought the urge to gather them with his lips.

She looked vulnerable and helpless. Yet he knew she had determination and courage. It rankled . . . the things he knew about her that he'd accepted so easily when he'd thought she was a boy. Now he was having to twist his thinking all around, and some things simply didn't want to be bent.

"I need the money bad," she said.

She no longer trembled. As a matter of fact, he was beginning to feel the warmth of her body easing through the dampness of her clothes to mingle with his. Her teeth no longer clacked and tiny shivers no longer cascaded through her. His reasons to hold her no longer existed.

"You okay now?" he asked gruffly.

She nodded slightly. "Yeah."

"Good." He eased her aside and stood. "Take off your shirt."

"What?" she asked, alarm rippling through her voice.

He snatched his shirt off the nearby bush. It was still damp in a few spots but for the most part it was dry. He tossed it onto her lap. "Put that on. I'm gonna go find your horse."

He started to stride away.

"Matt?"

He stilled and glanced back over his shoulder. With her hair plastered to her head, and her face still pale, she reminded him of a drowned kitten.

She licked her lips. "You gave me your word that you wouldn't tell anyone my secret."

"That's when I thought your secret was that you couldn't swim!" He was shaking almost as badly as she'd been. "I've got no choice, now that I know the truth. I have to tell Jake. You being a girl puts this whole operation in danger." He strode away, confusion dogging his heels.

Every time he looked at Sam, he'd get angry all over again. But he felt something else as well. Something he couldn't quite identify.

He'd developed a friendship with Sam. The thought of losing that hurt as deeply as her betrayal.

In bare feet, Sam sat on a log before the fire. She'd pulled off her boots and placed them close to the flames. Her shirt was now draped over the bush where Matt had put his earlier. She'd hung her britches there as well and wrapped the blanket securely around her.

It was going to be bad enough when they returned to the outfit and everyone learned she was a girl. She didn't want to be damp and shaking when she faced Jake. It had been awful, trembling in Matt's arms.

It had also been . . . comforting. Having him hold her. Her face had fit within the crook of his shoulder as though it belonged there. His arms around her had confirmed what she'd always suspected. He was strong, but also gentle.

She knew he was angry, understood that he had a right to be. She'd lied to him from the beginning. She'd cut her hair, spent close to six weeks trailing cattle—for what? They surely wouldn't pay her for the time she'd given them. Payment came at the end of the drive.

And she'd never see that day.

Besides, he'd warned her that Jake would brook no lies. And she'd lied every hour of every day . . . not with words, but with her disguise.

She knew beyond a doubt that Jake would send her packing . . . unless she could somehow convince Matt to keep her secret.

She heard footsteps and glanced up. Matt was leading Cinnamon into the clearing.

"Found her," he said without any emotion in his voice. He held up her jacket. "Found this, too."

He tossed it over the bush where her other clothes waited. He tethered Cinnamon to the low branch of a tree and wandered over to the fire. He hunkered down beside her and stared at the writhing flames.

His chest was still bared, and she remembered how warm it had been, how solid. She'd wanted to stay within his embrace until nightfall. Draw on his strength, his sturdiness.

But he'd dumped her off his lap as soon as he'd gotten her warm. And his vow to tell Jake the truth would get her kicked out of the outfit. She had to appeal to the part of him that had become her friend. "Matt?"

"Do you have any idea of what you've done?" He lunged to his feet and began to pace. "Jake trusted me."

He twisted around and glared at her. "Trusted my word. I told him to take you on." He plowed his hands through his hair. "He's gonna think I haven't got sense enough to spit downwind when he learns how you bamboozled me into believing you were a boy."

"Then don't tell him," Sam commanded.

"Did you get kicked in the head while you were struggling in the river?" he demanded.

Slowly she came to her feet. "I've been on this trail for six weeks. No one has figured it out. I can keep up the pretense for a few more weeks." She gave him a wry grin. "As long as I stay clear of rivers."

He obviously didn't appreciate her sorry excuse at humor as he glowered at her. "You can't stay. You're a girl."

"Which I've been all along!"

She took a step toward him and held out her hand. He looked at it as though she was offering him a snake. She lowered her hand to her side.

"Matt, I'm desperate. I didn't lie to you about how badly my family needs that hundred dollars." She grabbed her shorn locks. "I whacked off my hair. I've eaten grub and ridden drag until the dust nearly choked me, and I've never once complained. I'm a hard worker, Matt."

"I never said you weren't. But you're a girl! You lied to me, Sam. Every step of the way you lied to me."

His anger was palpable. She took a step back. "Would you have tried to convince Jake to take me on if you'd known I was a girl?" she asked.

"Heck fire no!"

"Which is exactly what I figured. So you gave me no choice but to hide the fact that I was a girl. Our pa died three years ago, the crops are barely making it. I've got a younger brother and sister . . . and my ma. The worry lines in her face run so deep now. I was desperate, Matt, desperate to get on this drive. I was willing to lie to anyone I needed to in order to accomplish that goal. Do anything that I had to do." Tentatively, she eased closer. "No one has to know that I'm a girl."

"I know," he ground out.

"Please, Matt—"

"I can't, Sam. It's bad luck to have a girl on a drive. I'm not going to be responsible for this drive failing."

"Coward!" she spat.

He jerked back as though she'd jabbed him. "I'm not a coward."

"Yes, you are. You're afraid of Jake, of what he might do. Maybe he'll let you go as well."

"He won't let me go. Unfortunately, he can't let you go,

either. At least, not right away." He looked defeated. "I was thinking about it while I was looking for your horse. We're miles from any town. There's no place close enough for him to kick you to."

Unwarranted relief coursed through her. She was getting a reprieve. She'd have a little more time to convince Matt to keep her secret. "So you're not going to tell him?"

"The crew knowing that you're a girl is just gonna cause trouble. I'll keep your secret until we get to a town, but then I'm telling and you're leaving." He stepped closer until they stood toe to toe. "Until then, though, you stay the heck away from me. You're on your own."

CHAPTER FOURTEEN

As the sun began to set, Matt urged his horse toward the main herd and the camp that he could see set up nearby. Beside him, Sam rode in silence. She hadn't spoken a single word since he'd stalked out of the clearing, demanding she leave him alone.

Which was exactly what he wanted. He didn't want her talking to him, looking at him, being friends with him.

How could he have been so gullible? How could he have not seen she was a girl?

Because he was certainly acutely aware of that fact now. Through the opening in her jacket, he could see the slight curves he'd never noticed before. Could remember how good it had felt to have them pressed against his chest as he'd worked to warm her.

"You'd better button up your jacket," he ordered.

She jerked as though he'd startled her, but she quickly did as he'd said.

"You're gonna have to cut your hair soon, too. With those curls getting longer, you look"—delicate, he thought; she looked delicate and lovely—"you just don't look so much like a boy."

She nodded. "I'll hack it off tonight. Thanks, Matt."

"Don't thank me," he barked. "I don't want Jake finding out that you're a girl until I'm good and ready to tell him, that's all. I have no plans to lose the respect he has for me. I've worked darned hard to earn it."

"So have I."

He glared at her. "I'm not saying you haven't, but you're a girl."

"You can still respect me."

"Not on a cattle drive, not when you've been lying to me the whole time."

"Matt, I've told you truths as well. Not everything about me is false."

"As far as I'm concerned it is."

He saw a horse kicking up dust and recognized its rider. Jake. Matt took a deep calming breath as the trail boss drew his horse to a halt. Matt knew he ought to be up front with Jake and reveal the truth, but he figured Jake would not only send Sam back, he'd make Matt go with her. And he needed to get her as far away from him as possible, as quickly as possible. At least until his temper died down and he could think straight.

"Took you long enough," Jake said. "Sam, anything broken?"

"Nothing," Matt replied before Sam could. Nothing broken except trust. "Sam was just a little shaken, so we took our time getting back."

"The best thing to do is just get back in the saddle," Jake told Sam.

Sam nodded. "That's what I aim to do, sir."

Matt wondered if Sam's voice had always sounded that soft. Or was he simply listening to Sam differently, looking at her with a clearer vision? The way her cheeks blushed when Jake spoke to her, the gentle arch of her eyebrows . . . and that mouth, that lying mouth that had definitely been shaped with kissing in mind.

Now, where had that thought come from?

"Matt?"

He jerked his gaze to Jake. "What?"

"You just looked like you were staring at nothing. Did you get hurt? Maybe take a kick to the head?"

Staring at nothing? He thought he might have been staring at the loveliest girl he'd ever laid eyes on. He shook his head briskly. "No, sir. Just got a little wet."

"Good. You two can take first watch," Jake said.

"Jake, I was just thinking that maybe Sam ought to . . ." Ought to what? "Ride with some other fella" was on the tip of his tongue, but what sort of trail hand would he be to place someone else in danger? Sam was his responsibility, more so now than ever.

Besides, Jake was glaring at him, waiting for some excuse that Matt couldn't form. "I think maybe Sam ought to rest up tonight. I'll take two watches to make up for someone else having to ride with me."

"All right. That's probably a good idea." Jake kicked his horse's flanks and the animal loped away.

"What in the heck did you do that for?" Sam asked.

"I figured you might still be shaken. A nervous rider can spook a cow and start a stampede."

"I'm not a nervous rider," Sam protested.

"Just take the night off," Matt ordered, "or I'll tell Jake the truth this very minute."

"I don't want you doing my share of the work."

"I won't. It's just that it's been a long day. Everyone will understand if you don't take a watch tonight. Let's get some grub." He urged his horse forward.

"Matt?"

He glanced over his shoulder and realized that there wasn't a solitary thing about Sam that resembled a boy. He could only hope that Jake didn't realize the truth before he had a chance to tell him.

"I never thanked you for coming to my rescue, for saving me from drowning."

He could do little more than nod brusquely and wonder who was going to save him from drowning within the green depths of her eyes.

Sam's favorite part of the evening came shortly after supper. The hands would begin settling in for the night. A couple of them brought out their harmonicas. Mouth organs, they called them. Sometimes they would play a familiar tune and one or two of the hands might provide the words. Sam often thought of singing, but she feared one of the men might listen more intently to her voice than Matt did when they were watching the cattle. Someone might realize she was a girl.

Someone besides Matt, that was. He had given her a bit of a reprieve and she intended to put the time to good use. She had no plans to leave this trail drive when Matt finally revealed her secret. She was determined to continue making herself useful and proving herself. Eventually, she would be needed to such a degree that Jake wouldn't think he could go on without her. She hadn't worked as hard as she had or suffered for as long as she had just so she could give it all up without a fight.

What sorts of dangers could there be? She hadn't caused anything to happen in the six weeks before this afternoon. Why would anything happen now?

With her back against the tree, she drew her knees up against her chest and wrapped her arms around her legs. She studied the men moving about camp. Some were only a little older than she was. Others looked considerably older. All gave her respect—because she was a hard worker, and because they thought she was a boy. Would it bother them to learn she was a girl?

She knew that it would. If she'd thought otherwise, she wouldn't have signed on under false pretenses to begin with. She wouldn't have chopped off her hair.

She supposed that Matt had a right to be angry. His reputation with the men—especially with Jake—was on the line. They probably would think he was gullible when they found out that she had convinced him she was a boy—convinced them all.

She tried not to remember how nice it had felt to be pressed against him this afternoon. His body had been warm, his arms strong.

She'd been struggling within the churning water, almost in a panic. Until she'd heard his voice, caught sight of him scrambling across the backs of the cows. Coming to her rescue.

She'd known without a doubt then that she'd be all right. Matt would save her.

She supposed she owed him. She figured that the decent thing to do would be to pack up her belongings and leave quietly, peacefully, before he had to tell anyone, before he had to embarrass himself. She could just drift away into the night, never to be heard from again. Years from now, on other cattle drives, the cowboys would talk about that boy Sam who had turned into a first-rate cowpuncher . . . and then was gone. Like smoke blowing away into the dark.

If only she didn't need a hundred dollars so badly, she might leave. If only her family wasn't depending on her. Then maybe she could spare Matt the embarrassment.

As it was, she would have to risk it, risk everything, on the slight chance that when all was said and done, Jake, and even Matt, would see her as a dependable cowboy—instead of a troublesome girl.

The Big Dipper had rotated around so it hung beneath the North Star by the time that Matt wandered into camp following his second shift. He was bone-weary and dead tired. Rescuing Sam had taken more out of him than he'd realized. He was glad that he'd suggested she stay in camp tonight. She had to be more exhausted than he was.

Her panic had been more evident, her fear more obvious.

He pulled his bedroll out of the back of the wagon and slowly let his gaze circle the clearing, identifying the trail hands who were stretched out sleeping. He spotted Sam and his breath backed up in his lungs.

She reminded him of a lonely, little kitten, curled up so far from the others. He understood now why she'd kept herself aloof. She must have constantly worried that she'd give herself away.

He considered sleeping on the opposite side of the camp from her, but folks would wonder what had happened between them, why he was suddenly avoiding her. So he couldn't take that approach. He'd just have to steel himself against noticing her. He'd just have to pretend that she was a boy.

But as he crossed the camp and crouched beside her, he knew that task was going to be impossible. Lying on her side, she had one hand pressed beneath her cheek and the other resting against her stomach. She had such delicate-looking hands.

Her hands intrigued him because he also knew they were capable. She could guide her horse, herd the cattle. A couple of her nails were chipped and broken. It might have happened when she was saddling her horse or gathering wood for the fire. How had she managed to heft the saddle onto her horse's back?

In sleep, she'd parted her mouth slightly, but she didn't snore, like all the other fellas. She was quiet. If any breath passed between her lips at all, it was silent. He wondered if those lips felt as soft as they looked.

Her eyelashes fluttered, and then she opened her eyes. The night shadows hid the green depths from him, but still he knew they were there, knew the exact shade.

"What are you doing?" she asked in a sleepy voice that slammed hard into his gut.

"Figured I'd best bed down beside you so the fellas don't start asking me why I'm mad enough to spit nails, avoiding you," he explained as he quickly went about setting up his bedroll. "We just have to pretend nothing has changed."

And that was going to be close to impossible, he thought, as he stretched out beside her. He went to toe off his boots and froze. Lying beside a girl with socks showing seemed incredibly intimate, even though he'd done it close to forty nights already. Somehow, he couldn't bring himself to do it tonight.

He glanced down at her feet. She was still wearing her boots as well. He shoved his hands beneath his head and glared at the sky. He was so tired that he should have had no trouble getting to sleep. As it was, he was wound up tighter than a rope tossed around an escaping calf and jerked taut.

"Matt, I'm sorry," she said softly.

Her voice went right through him, reached out to touch all the lonely spots. That ability of hers to make him want to protect her irritated the devil out of him. "It's a little late for sorry."

"Haven't you ever done something that you didn't want to do, but you knew you had to do it?"

He ground his teeth together, trying not to think about the war, the many things he'd done that he hadn't wanted to do. The fields he'd marched out onto, the bullets he'd fired, the enemy he'd killed.

"Matt, I know you're honorable and anything you've done you've done because you thought it was best at the time."

He turned his head and stared at her. "Sam, you're not going to sweet-talk me into changing my mind. It's because I'm trying to look after you that I have to tell Jake the truth when the time is right."

"My sister Amy has never worn a dress that I didn't wear first. My brother Nate goes to bed hungry. My ma is all hunched over with the burdens she carries."

He turned his attention back to the stars. He didn't want to hear the unspoken plea in her voice to hold her secret close to his chest and not tell anyone.

"Matt, you've told me repeatedly that I was doing a good job. I'm not going to stop working hard. I didn't just suddenly turn into a girl this afternoon."

"You sure as heck did as far as I'm concerned." He rolled onto his side and faced her. "Sam, a cattle drive is no place for a girl. Look at what happened today."

"Are you saying that no *cowboy* ever slid off his horse into the river?"

"What I'm saying is that Jake made you my responsibility and taking care of a *girl* is not what I signed up to do!" he hissed through clenched teeth. "Now, go to sleep before I decide to tell Jake the truth at sunup."

Her eyes shot daggers at him before she turned and gave him her back. A slender back. He remembered how dainty she'd felt in his arms. He did not want to think about the frailty of her bones or the warmth of her skin.

He didn't want to remember holding her . . . and he sure as heck didn't want to wonder what it would feel like to kiss her, to plant his mouth against hers . . .

Frustrated by his wandering thoughts, he rolled onto

his side and glared at the small fire in the center of camp. His body was growing as hot as the flames.

If the river had been within walking distance, he'd have headed for it and dived headfirst into it.

As it was, he stayed awake all night thinking about Sam the *girl* and wishing that he didn't have to tell Jake the truth.

But he had to. Keeping the truth to himself wasn't fair to Jake, the men, or the Broken Heart ranch.

CHAPTER FIFTEEN

Sam shoved her bedroll into the supply wagon. Fighting the turbulent waters of the river had left her battered and bruised. Fighting Matt had left her unaccountably sad.

She enjoyed riding with the herd, felt a sense of accomplishment far greater than any she'd felt as she'd worked the farm. It shouldn't matter to Matt or Jake that she was a girl. As long as she could do the tasks assigned to her, it shouldn't matter at all that she was female. It certainly didn't make one bit of difference to the cows.

She had to find a way to convince Matt not to reveal her secret. He needed to give her the opportunity to finish this drive.

Turning, she jumped back, startled. Matt stood there, both his horse and hers in tow.

"Got your horse ready," he said as he handed her the reins.

"I can saddle my own horse," she spat in a low voice as she jerked them from his grasp.

"I know. It's just that I was saddling mine so I thought I'd go ahead and saddle yours."

She narrowed her eyes. "Matt, you can't treat me

differently just because you know I'm a girl."

"I don't intend to, but neither am I going to treat you like you're a boy!" he hissed in a low voice.

"You're making me mad, you know that?"

She mounted her horse, and with a gentle kick to the animal's sides, urged Cinnamon toward the herd. She yanked her bandanna up over her nose. Today she'd be grateful that she was riding drag and wouldn't have an opportunity to talk with Matt.

The cattle were starting their slow plodding north. They usually grazed as they went in the morning and would begin to move a little more quickly as the day wore on.

Out of the corner of her eye, Sam caught sight of Matt drawing his horse up beside hers. She didn't want to notice the breadth of his shoulders or the strength in his hands.

"There's no reason you have to keep riding beside me," she told him. "I've been at this six weeks now. I'm comfortable with it. Tell Jake to move you on up to point."

Beneath the brim of his hat, his blue eyes widened. "Are you crazy? You're my responsibility."

"I can watch the back end of cattle without your help," she insisted.

"Until Jake orders me to ride point, I'm riding beside you."

She watched his bandanna riffle with his breath as he spoke. Days on a drive were usually long and arduous. She had a feeling they were going to get much worse.

Suddenly Matt sat up straighter in the saddle, his gaze focused on the far horizon.

"What is it?" Sam asked.

"Looks like smoke."

She glanced around. "What's out here to burn? Thought you said there were no towns."

"There's grass. Without it, we might as well turn around and head home, because the cattle would have nothing to eat. You stay here."

She chafed at his order, but obeyed. She watched as he galloped toward the smoke rising in the east. She saw other trail hands riding after him. Then she spotted the supply wagon headed in that direction.

Jeb and Jed joined her. "What's going on?" they asked as one.

"Matt thinks it's a prairie fire," she explained.

"Sure looks like it, with that black smoke billowing," Jed said. Or was it Jeb? She never knew.

"Thank goodness the wind is blowing away from us. If the cattle caught the scent, they'd start stampeding. You and Jed hightail it out there to help 'em put it out," Jeb said. "I've got the most experience with a herd. I can keep these little doggies in line."

She thought about pointing out that Matt had ordered her to stay put, but Matt wasn't her keeper. He thought he was but she knew differently. She could handle herself out here. Besides, he might not have realized how bad the fire was when he issued that order.

Giving Jeb a quick nod, she kicked her horse's flanks and followed Jed, who hadn't taken time trying to decide whether or not fighting the fire was what needed to be done.

By the time they arrived at the supply wagon, Cookie was already soaking gunny sacks in the barrel of rainwater and passing them off to the men. From what Sam could tell as she dismounted, it looked as though about three-fourths of the men were here. She could see Matt pounding at the flames on one side of the fire.

"It's a small one, fellas," Cookie told them as he passed each man a drenched sack. "Let's keep it that way. Beat it out from the sides and work your way to the middle."

With unexpected excitement, Sam grabbed the sack that Cookie extended toward her. No one was questioning her right to be here. Matt might have doubts regarding her abilities, but none of the other trail hands did.

To ensure that Matt didn't interfere, however, she went to the side opposite from where he stood. The thick smoke was billowing up; sparks danced wildly in the haze. She heard the crackle of the fire as it devoured the dry prairie grasses and the thud of the gunny sacks slapped at the ground, beating down the writhing, twisting flames.

She took her cue from the men around her, periodically dashing to the wagon to dip her sack quickly into the water before rushing back to the fire with her dripping burden. Her arms began to ache as she pounded the earth with the sack. The soot and ash stung her eyes and coated her clothes.

But still she beat at the flames over and over and over, refusing to be defeated, wondering briefly if this fearful exhilaration was what soldiers experienced as they marched into war.

To know that she was needed, to know that she was making a difference. Matt was going to destroy all she'd worked incredibly hard to attain.

And when he did, whatever affection she might have harbored for him would die. And she'd despise him for as long as she drew breath.

"Make sure all the sparks are dead!" Matt yelled as he pounded the final flames into submission. He knew too well how quickly a single spark could re-ignite a dying fire.

This prairie fire hadn't been the worst he'd ever seen. He figured it had burned for only a mile or so. He was extremely grateful that it was upwind of the cattle and hadn't caused them to start stampeding.

What had started the fire could have been anyone's guess. A careless cowboy driving a herd ahead of theirs might have dropped an unlit match. All it took was a bird pecking at it to create a spark. A spark that had erupted into a prairie fire. He'd known of it happening before.

He gazed at the blackened earth that was still smoldering. Thin wisps of smoke continued to curl upward. Add the burdensome task of killing the fire to his double watch last night and his rescuing Sam in the river yesterday . . . and he was nearly tuckered out. And the sun wasn't even directly overhead yet.

"Good work!" Jake shouted as he rode around the darkened perimeter, inspecting for sparks.

Men barely spoke as they trudged toward the wagon and the waiting horses. Above their bandannas, their faces were covered with soot. Some were barely recognizable. He smiled at the sight of Sam. She looked like a raccoon.

Sam!

What in thunderation was she doing here?

"Hey, Sam!" he yelled.

She stopped walking. His heart had been pumping madly as he'd fought to put out the fire. He knew the dangers of a prairie fire. Out of control, it could destroy all in its path, including the herd. And if the cattle were spared, but the grass burned . . . they'd have nothing for the steers to eat. The animals would have perished, and all their weeks of laborious work would have been for nothing.

Yet during the entire battle of man against nature, as Matt had worked to put out the fire, he hadn't shaken. Not like he was trembling now. Just the thought of the dangers she'd exposed herself to had his knees growing weak.

"I ordered you to stay with the herd!" he snapped, when he got close enough to see the green in her eyes.

"I was needed here!" she retorted.

"I told you to keep the heck away!" He came to an abrupt halt. He didn't know whether to throttle her for disobeying an order or hug her because she'd managed not to get hurt.

"I figured you didn't realize how bad the fire was," she said.

"I knew exactly how bad it was. That's why I didn't want you over here."

"What's going on?" Jake asked, as he brought his horse to a halt beside them. A cowboy never walked when he could ride.

Matt pointed his shaking finger at Sam. "She . . . shee-eeez . . . I—I told Sam to stay with the herd." Dang it! He'd almost said, "*She* was supposed to stay with the herd."

"Sam was right to come over here. We needed as many men as possible to get this fire put out. We couldn't risk it burning out of control or getting close enough to spook the cattle."

"But Sam's not a man!" he yelled and saw the dread pop into Sam's widening eyes. "He . . . he's a boy."

"There are no boys on this drive. Sam did a heck of a fine job," Jake said.

Matt thought Sam was going to bust the buttons on her shirt as she puffed out her chest with pride. Those buttons popping off would surely cause problems. "But he disobeyed an order."

"You've been to war, Matt. You know sometimes the man giving the orders doesn't always give the best orders," Jake said.

Matt jerked his gaze to Jake's. Jake tilted his head slightly. "Leave the boy be, Matt. He did what was best for the outfit. You gotta respect that." He grinned at Sam. "You're turning out to be quite a surprise."

Matt thought Jake had no idea how close he was to speaking the absolute truth.

As Jake sent his horse into a canter, Matt glanced tentatively back at Sam. She'd pulled her bandanna down so it hung loosely around her neck, and she was beaming with satisfaction at the praise Jake had bestowed upon her.

She should have looked ridiculous with half her face blackened and that giddy-looking smile . . . instead, he thought she looked beautiful.

And he finally figured out that he didn't want to throttle her and he didn't want to hug her. He wanted to kiss her.

* * *

Sam allowed the tranquillity of the vast midnight sky to ease into her soul. These moments when she rode night guard were some of her favorite. The cattle's lowing was as much a lullaby as the songs she sang to them.

Sitting on the ground, they didn't stir up dust. Not even when they occasionally awkwardly got to their feet, turned, and worked their way back to the ground.

The prairie at night was breathtaking. After trailing the cattle mile after monotonous mile during the day, she anticipated her two-hour night watch. Even Matt's foul mood as he rode beside her couldn't dampen her spirits.

She had certainly proven her worth today. Maybe Jake wouldn't mind so much when he discovered the truth about her. For a harrowing minute this afternoon, she'd thought that Matt had almost given away the fact that she was a girl. He'd certainly done some quick tripping over his tongue. She'd never seen him so furious, not even by the river yesterday.

Riding along beside her, he was still moping. He hadn't spoken a single word to her since Jake had praised her, and they had all rejoined the herd.

Matt had taken his meal away from the campfire, causing the others to look at him in an odd way. They were probably trying to figure out why he was so riled. Squirrel had said that Sam disobeying an order couldn't be what was setting him off. The others had started speculating, wondering if he had a burr in his britches or a blister on his foot.

She thought she'd go crazy if he kept up this silent treatment. It was such a peaceful night, a good time for mending fences.

"I love herding cattle at night," she said quietly. "I find it calming."

Silence. Heavy, palpable. Thick enough to slice with a butter knife.

"I reckon we're really lucky that the cattle didn't stampede this morning."

Nothing from him. Not even a turn of his head.

"Have you gone deaf?" she snapped.

The only thing worse than being yelled at was being ignored.

"How long do you plan to stay angry?" she asked.

"Forever."

The pain cut into her like a rusty bayonet. She didn't want to admit how much she'd come to like him, to care about him.

In her heart, she knew that his attempt to guard her was the reason he'd ordered her to stay away from the fire. It wasn't that he'd thought her incapable; it was that he'd worried she'd get hurt.

"If I'd confessed that I was a girl when we were behind

the general store, you never would have put in a good word for me with Jake. I needed this chance, Matt, I needed to be able to bring some hope to my family that the bad times were behind us."

Within the night shadows, she saw him turn his head toward her. Hope spiraled in her that he was truly listening, that he would come to understand why she'd done all she had.

She could feel his gaze boring into her. Licking her lips, she swallowed hard. "If you tell Jake the truth about me, he's gonna send me packing. I don't care about me, but I do care about my family doing without, my mother worrying about the debt mounting at the general store. I know you hate me for deceiving you. But please don't take your hatred for me out on my family. Please don't tell Jake that I'm a girl."

Leaning over in the saddle, he reached out and cupped the back of her head. Then his mouth swooped down to cover hers, hard, desperate, hot. Incredibly hot. Like the flames they'd battled this afternoon.

Warmth sluiced through her body like hot maple syrup being poured over flapjacks.

Breathing heavily, he pulled back. "*That's* the reason you can't stay. I can't stop thinking about you, wanting to hold you, desperate to kiss you."

With her lips swollen and still tingling, she stared at

him. He wanted to kiss her?

"From the moment we saddled up today, I've thought only about you. I haven't thought about the cattle. And that's too dangerous. If the other men start doing the same thing, someone is going to get hurt. Or worse, killed."

CHAPTER SIXTEEN

Three days later, Matt was still thinking about that kiss. It had come as no surprise that Sam's lips were incredibly soft. As he tossed his saddle over his horse's back, he realized that what had surprised him was that she hadn't shoved him away.

He cinched the saddle into place. She was a lady. He could see it in the way she ate . . . delicately, slowly taking the spoon of stew to her mouth. Not shoveling the food in, like the other trail hands did. She never talked around a biscuit. She never belched to show her appreciation of a meal.

She was so danged female that he was grateful trailing a herd left men too weary to notice much of anything except the slow passing of the minutes.

The jangling of spurs had him glancing over his shoulder. Jake was coming toward him like there was no tomorrow.

"Is there a reason Sam can't saddle his own horse?" Jake asked brusquely.

Matt shrugged. "Sam's my partner. I have to saddle my horse. Might as well get his ready."

"It's not a good idea to spoil a fella," Jake admonished.

"Just doing a good deed."

"Then you can do another good deed. I want you to ride up to the next river, take a look-see, and determine if we need to guide the cattle over slow or fast. If they had heavy snows up in Colorado, they'll be melting by now and it'll affect the rivers here. If the water's high, we'll spread the cattle out, take 'em over slow. If it's low, we'll bunch 'em together and get them across fast. You ought to be able to get there before nightfall. Just camp by the river and head back at first light. That ought to give us enough time to determine how to move the cattle."

Matt nodded, even though he had reservations about leaving Sam. He considered suggesting that Jake give the task to someone else, but he was supposed to be learning on this trip so he could serve as trail boss on the next one or the one after that.

Sam was distracting him from his mission. He ought to be spending more time talking with Jake, learning from him. "Will do."

"Take Sam with you."

Matt's stomach dropped clear down to his boots. Him and Sam alone . . . on the prairie . . . at night? Not if his life depended on it. "I'm not sure that's such a good idea."

Jake arched a brow. "Why not?"

"Sam's such a greenhorn—"

"And he's going to stay a greenhorn if he doesn't start pulling his weight."

"She—sheez . . . he—he pulls his weight. You said so yourself when Sam fought the fire."

"And ever since that day, there's been something going on between you and Sam."

Matt's breath backed up into his lungs until his chest ached. What was his attitude toward Sam revealing? "What do you mean?"

"I can't quite figure it out. He looks at you like you're a rattler about to strike and you're watching him like you're expecting horns to sprout out of his head at any minute. The way you two are dancing around each other is making the men and the cattle nervous. Your pa is expecting you to learn how to lead this bunch. You can start by resolving whatever differences you're having with Sam."

Matt stood rooted to the spot as Jake strode away. It was the difference between him and Sam that was causing the problems.

The difference being that Sam had curves where Matt didn't.

Sam tried to ignore the fella riding beside her—dismiss him just as diligently as he was ignoring her. Closing her eyes, she tilted her head back so the sun could touch her face. She'd almost forgotten what it was like to ride an entire day without a bandanna covering her face. Without dust rising up from the tread of two thousand cattle to coat her clothing and any exposed skin.

She felt downright giddy. She wasn't going to let Matt spoil her day away from the cantankerous beasts. And tonight there'd be no cattle to watch. As calming as she found the night shift, she was looking forward to sleeping through the night without being awakened with a quietly murmured, "It's time."

"Stop doing that," Matt ordered.

She snapped her eyes open and looked at him. "Doing what?"

"Looking like . . . *I* don't know. Looking like you just stepped into paradise."

"Just because you were raised on sour milk doesn't mean that I have to act like I was," she retorted, tilting her nose in the air.

"The milk I was raised on has nothing to do with my disposition. The responsibility for that lies entirely with your deception."

"Aren't you getting tired of harping on me lying to you back in Faithful? Why can't you forgive me for telling you I was a boy?"

"Because your lie put us in danger."

"Honestly, Matt, I don't see how my being a girl is hurting anyone. No one is sick or bleeding. No one is dying. I'm doing my job. Doing it well, according to Jake."

"The problem, Sam, is that I'm not doing mine."

"*The* problem then is *your* problem. Just stop thinking of me as a girl," she said.

He raked his gaze over her. "That's a little hard to do."

"So is doing without and going hungry and being cold in winter."

He averted his gaze. "I'm responsible for you, Sam."

"I don't need you looking out for me. I can be responsible for myself." Why couldn't he get that notion through his thick skull? She supposed she should admire his dogged determination to take care of her, but his obsession was keeping her from reaching her goal.

"As soon as we're close enough to a town that I can get you to safely and you can catch a stagecoach home, I'm telling Jake the truth," Matt said.

"I'll hate you when you do that."

He gave her a sad smile. "Then that'll make two of us who hate me. But if I learned one thing during the war, Sam, it was that I had to do what I thought was best for the boys in my command. Otherwise, they'd haunt me. I'd never forgive myself if anything happened to you . . . or if anything happened to any of the trail hands because I hadn't come forward and told Jake that I knew you were a girl."

She heaved a heavy sigh. "How far is the nearest town?"

"Now, *that* I'm not sure about."

She would hope it was Sedalia. If they got the cattle to Missouri, then surely they'd pay her. And that was all she really wanted. To be paid.

And if she never set eyes on Matt again afterward— it would be too soon.

* * *

The river didn't look swollen or treacherous, but Matt knew things weren't always as they appeared. Sam had taught him that painful lesson.

With the sun retreating so the night could begin casting its shadows over the land, Matt neared the bank. He studied the flow of the river. He knew he should test the waters by riding his horse across, but he wasn't in the mood to spend the night in drenched britches. And he couldn't shuck them with Sam sitting on her horse beside him.

"You think it's safe?" she asked.

"Looks it, but I need to check the current out more closely to be sure. Close your eyes."

"Why?"

He glared at her. "Because I'm stripping down."

Her cheeks burned bright crimson and she released a tiny "Oh."

"I don't want to get my clothes wet," he explained.

She nodded briskly. "I understand."

"Do you, Sam? Do you realize that I wouldn't have this problem if you were a boy?"

"You don't have the problem now. I've already seen your bare backside!"

Now Matt's face grew hot. "Well, you wouldn't have if I'd known the truth. Now, close your eyes," he ordered as he dismounted.

"I'll do you one better. I'll just mosey on out of your

way." Sam urged her horse toward the distant brush until they were out of his sight.

As Matt grabbed his horse's reins and ducked behind the trees, he should have felt more comfortable. Instead, he felt his skin turning three shades of red as he thought about how he'd removed his clothes that first evening. He'd certainly given her an eyeful then.

He took off his clothes, feeling as vulnerable as a newborn baby. He mounted his horse and gave him a good, solid kick to prod him forward. The more quickly he went into the river, the faster he could get out and put his clothes back on.

It wasn't until he was calf-deep into the river that he realized Sam hadn't agreed to close her eyes. She'd only offered to get out of the way.

Sam hadn't meant to spy on Matt. She'd dismounted and was walking her horse farther away when Cinnamon had simply nudged Sam's backside with her nose. Sam had turned to admonish the mare—and caught sight of Matt sitting on his horse like a marble statue she'd seen in a book at school. All hard lines and carved muscles.

She couldn't blame him for not wanting to get his clothes wet. Apparently he hadn't brought extras, while she had given a lot of thought to being near a river with no one around except Matt.

Matt, who knew she was a girl. Once he had his time

alone in the river, she had plans to have a few private moments in it as well. She'd brought clean clothes for the occasion.

Matt still wore his cowboy hat. It sent shade over his bronzed back. The river appeared calm, but a few hundred cattle had the power to send the waters to swirling. And they had close to two thousand.

She considered turning away and giving Matt his privacy, but now that she was watching him, she decided it was for the best. What if he slipped off the saddle? She needed to be prepared to rescue him. Jake probably expected them to watch out for each other.

Halfway across the river, the water was lapping at Matt's thighs. Slowly, he turned his horse around and headed back toward shore.

With a sigh of relief, she spun on the balls of her feet and began to pay a good deal of attention to her own horse. No need for him to know that she'd been admiring him.

"Why don't you start gathering some dry driftwood and such for a fire?" Matt yelled from behind a tree. "I'll scare us up a rabbit for dinner."

"How was the current?" she asked as he broke through the brush, horse in tow.

"Not too strong. We should be able to get the cattle across without as much trouble as we had at the last passing." He held her gaze. "Are you gonna be all right crossing the river?"

"Sure." If her stomach would loosen up a notch or two.

"I'll see to the horses before I find us something to eat."

"Matt, I can see to my own horse," she told him.

He rubbed the side of his nose. "I know you can, but as long as we're out here away from the others, I don't have to pretend that you're a boy. And since that is the case, I've decided to treat you like a lady. So I'll see to both horses."

"You need to be careful that you don't develop bad habits while we're out here. I don't want anyone figuring out that I'm not a boy," she said.

"I've already gotten into some bad habits where you're concerned," he admitted.

"Such as?"

"Bedding down each night and thinking about that durned kiss." He turned on his heel and strode away.

Unfortunately for her, she'd developed the same bad habit.

CHAPTER SEVENTEEN

Wicked. Sam felt terribly wicked as she sank into the river. Ever since Matt had told her that they were going to check out the next river—and camp beside it—she'd thought of nothing else but shedding her clothing and getting rid of the dirt.

She dipped beneath the water. For once she was grateful that her hair was short so it wasn't swirling around her in the river. Coming back to the surface, she began to lather up the small sliver of perfumed soap she'd hoarded during the war. She had brought it with her, expecting to use it at journey's end. She used it only on special occasions. Other times she used the lye soap her mother made. She had decided that this evening called for using her special soap.

Tonight she didn't have to watch the way she walked, the way she talked, the way her clothes covered her body, or the way she looked at Matt. Tonight she could be a girl.

For much of her life, she'd resented the fact that she couldn't do all the things that her brothers could. Couldn't go to war, couldn't go on a cattle drive. Wasn't supposed to climb trees or spit.

Now that she was pretending to be a boy, she missed being a girl. She missed wearing a dress, plaiting long hair, smelling sweet.

She scrubbed her scalp. All those shorn curls felt strange. Men on cattle drives didn't seem overly concerned with cleanliness, which worked to her advantage as far as hiding herself, but she couldn't say it was a way of life she'd want for long. Most of the men acted as though they were plumb shy of water and soap.

Matt seemed to be an exception. Every Saturday night he took a razor to his face to scrape away his beard—not that he had much of one to scrape away. It intrigued her, though. In truth, just about everything about him did.

She dunked her head beneath the water and rinsed away the soap before bursting through to the surface. The moon reflected off the rippling waters. The wind whispered through the trees lining the bank.

Kicking up her feet, she floated on her back. She couldn't remember ever feeling this relaxed, as though somehow, in some way, everything would turn out right.

"What in tarnation do you think you're doing?" Matt yelled.

Sam bobbed upright, her feet hitting the muddy bottom with such force that she slipped, lost her balance, and went under. She came up sputtering. Flicking the water out of her eyes, she saw a rush of movement in the water. Matt had obviously thought she was in trouble and was coming to her rescue again. "Stop!" she screamed.

Drenched, Matt came to an abrupt halt and stood. The water lapped around his waist. "Are you all right?" he asked.

"Yes," she answered, trying to calm her pounding heart. He was standing too close. She kept her shoulders submerged. "What are you doing out here?"

"You said you were going to come wash up. I started to get worried. I didn't think it would take you so long to wash your face and hands. But now I can see that you planned to wash more than that," he said gruffly.

A tingle of pleasure speared her with his confession. He'd been thinking of her. She wondered if his thoughts about her wandered along the same paths as her thoughts about him.

"You didn't have to worry. I just wanted to feel clean," she said. She skimmed her hand across the surface of the water, spraying him.

"Hey!" he yelled.

She swam back a ways. "I don't know how you cowboys can go so long without bathing."

"Wait right there," he ordered and started trudging away from her.

"What are you going to do?" she asked.

"Take off my clothes and join you."

"You can't do that!" she shouted at his retreating back.

"Sure I can. But don't worry. I'll stay on my half of the river."

He became lost in the shadows. Suddenly she felt very, very naughty. Before the war, she was certain Benjamin had gone swimming with people his own age . . . girls and boys. They kept a respectful distance from each other. It was just the way things were done.

She heard a splash and abruptly Matt broke through the surface of the water a few yards away from her. He swept his hair out of his eyes before flicking some water at her.

"I don't want to fight, Matt," she said quietly.

"Neither do I."

She swam away from him. "We probably shouldn't be doing this."

"Probably not," he admitted. "I can't see anything, Sam. Except shadows."

"You ever gone swimming with a girl before?" she asked.

"A time or two."

Jealousy reared its ugly head. She didn't want to think of him in the water with another girl.

He swam toward the middle of the river. "Have you ever been swimming with a fella?" he asked.

She considered lying, but she was tired of all the lies between them. She wanted to strengthen their precarious friendship with truths.

"No." She bobbed in the water. "I'd always get envious when you or one of the hands would jump into a watering hole."

He stilled. "I never considered how hard it would be for you never to be able to take a swim without fear of being seen . . . or caught."

She watched as his silhouette plowed his hands through his hair.

"I'm not upset about it," she explained. "I understand that's the way it needs to be."

"Most cowboys don't bathe till the end of the drive," he said.

"Why don't you wait?" she asked.

"Can't stand all the dirt, reminds me of the war. Not as much as a river does, though."

"What do you mean?" she asked.

"During the war, we'd camp by a river as often as possible. At night, it gets so peaceful. We'd be on one side, Yankees on the other. Some fella would start playing on his mouth organ, then someone on the other side of the river might start to sing. We'd forget for a while that we were enemies. Kinda like you and I are doing now."

Her stomach knotted. "I've never thought of you as my enemy, Matt."

"Even though I'm gonna tell Jake the truth . . . as soon

as the time is right?" he asked.

She took a deep breath. She considered begging, pleading, offering him a portion of her earnings . . . but instead she offered him the truth. "I'll admit that I wish you wouldn't tell him. My reasons for coming on this drive haven't changed. I think I'm a fair trail hand. I know I wouldn't be here if you hadn't intervened, and I owe you for that. I wish I hadn't had to lie to you, but sometimes we have no choice. We have to do things we don't want to do."

He pounded the river with his fist and sent up a stream of water. "Why do you have to say and do things that make me like you? Why can't you throw a hissy fit so I'll be glad to get rid of you?"

A tingle of joy coursed through her, and she smiled slightly. "I thought you would be glad to be rid of me."

"I like you, Sam. I mean, you learn fast, you work hard, you never complain . . . except when I try to stop you from doing something. You're the kinda girl that makes a fella think he might welcome Cupid's cramps."

Her smile grew. "Cupid's cramps"—a cowboy's name for love. She didn't know why fellas had to act as though taking a liking to a girl was the most awful thing that could happen to them.

"Speaking of Cupid's cramps," he said, speculation laced through his voice, "that night when we went to that dance . . . you were in such a strange mood. You didn't like me dancing with those girls, did you?"

"Not particularly. I wanted you to dance with me," she admitted.

She shivered as the breeze blew off the bank. She didn't really want to talk about how jealous she'd been that night. It made her feel small and petty, after all he'd done for her.

"I'm starting to wrinkle from being in here so long," she announced.

"Go on and get out. I won't look," he said, just before he dived into the water.

She waded through the river, toward the shore, not exactly certain what had happened between them. Or why it had happened.

But suddenly she felt as though she and Matt were friends again . . . closer than they'd been before.

Matt waited until he was certain he'd given Sam enough time to get clear of the water and don her clothes. Then he swam to the shore and slipped on his own damp britches and shirt. He'd seen her slide beneath the water and his heart had leaped into his throat at the same time that he'd dived into the river.

The girl was going to be the death of him yet. Funny thing was, he didn't mind coming to her aid. He knew he was actually going to miss her sass when she was gone.

Picking up his boots, he headed back to camp. Jake had been right. He and Sam needed to reconcile their differences, but Matt wasn't certain that Jake realized exactly what he was asking of Matt.

Matt strode into camp. Sam had set up their pallets on opposite sides of the fire. She was already lying on hers. He grinned. To watch her through the night, he'd have to stare through the flames. "You didn't have to set up a place for me."

"Why not? You tended to my horse," she said with that little chin of hers thrust up at an obstinate angle.

He crouched before the fire to get some of the chill, caused by the damp clothes, off his body. He rubbed his hands together. "I've decided that I'm not gonna tell Jake," he said quietly.

She sat bolt upright, as though he'd tossed a rattler onto her lap. "What?"

He shook his head and sighed heavily. "You *are* a good trail hand. You need the money. We've only got a few weeks left until we reach Sedalia. I reckon your secret can hold till then."

"Oh, Matt!" She flung her arms around him and sent him flying backward, landing with a thud on the hard ground while her small body was sprawled over his larger one.

Her heaving chest pressed against his. She was so

warm. Even through his clothes, he could feel her warmth. She pushed off him. Her cheeks burned as brightly as the flames in the fire as she scrambled back and sat on her pallet.

"I'm obliged. Why did you change your mind?" she asked.

"I don't know. I just figured you've been a girl since we left Faithful and nothing bad has happened. We'll just hope your luck continues."

Besides, he didn't want to see her leave. But he sure as heck couldn't tell her that. He had to keep some distance between them——for her sake *and* his. He unfolded his body and gathered up his bedding.

"What are you doing?" she asked.

"Gonna move to the other side of you." He walked around and dropped down beside her.

"Why?"

"With a fire, it's unlikely animals will attack, but if they do, I want to be between them and you."

She rolled her eyes. "Matt——"

"Don't argue with me, Sam, or I'll tell Jake the truth."

She narrowed her eyes and then relented. "Fine."

He stretched out beside her. It wasn't unusual for folks to sleep side by side. People attending a dance might stay the night and stretch out on the floor, not caring that they weren't married to the person they were lying beside. Even stagecoach inns sometimes bedded complete strangers together.

A fragrance teased his nostrils. He raised up on an elbow and gazed at Sam. "What's that flowery smell?"

He watched her cheeks turn a pinkish hue, and he didn't think the heat of the fire was responsible.

"Some soap I use on special occasions. I was tired of smelling like a steer . . . I just decided to use it tonight. The scent will be gone tomorrow. No one will notice."

"That first night when I went to wake you, I noticed that you smelled like flowers. I just figured you'd held your ma tightly when you said good-bye. But now I reckon that's just the way you smell, isn't it?"

"When I haven't gone weeks without a good hot bath."

"That scent could spook the cattle," he mused as he skimmed his fingers over her hair. It sure spooked him, deep down inside where he was trying to ignore her. "How long was your hair before you chopped it off?"

"Down to my waist. But it'll grow back."

"I'll bet it was pretty." He could envision the flames from the fire sending their light dancing over the auburn tresses.

"My ma called it my crowning glory."

"I'd like to see it sometime after it grows back." He trailed his finger along her temple, over her cheek. She looked so feminine. How in the world had he ever considered she was a boy? "Do folks call you 'Sam'?"

"Most call me Samantha Jane. Does everyone call you 'Matt'?"

He grinned. "Unless they're mad at me. Then it's Matthew."

"I should probably call you Matthew, then, since you make me angry a good deal of the time."

His grin grew as he held her gaze. "I like the way it sounds when you say it."

"Matthew," she repeated, with a shy smile hovering on her lips.

Sparks from the fire crackled and popped into the air, waltzing back to the ground. A calmness settled over him. He hadn't felt this way since long before the war. As though everything would be all right.

She had such pretty eyes. Her gaze was wandering over his face as though she was trying to memorize the curves and lines. He wished he'd brought his razor with him, but it was with his other supplies in the wagon. He had three days' worth of beard. It wasn't thick. He couldn't even call it bristly. Still, it shadowed his face.

Impulsively, he reached out and cradled her cheek with his hand and grazed his thumb over her lips. He heard her breath hitch.

"Samantha Jane." He liked the way her name rolled off his tongue. "When I kissed you before, I was mad that I wanted to kiss you."

She nodded slightly, her eyes never leaving his. "I figured as much."

"I'm not mad now."

He saw her swallow. "You're not?"

He lowered his head and kissed one corner of her mouth and then the other. "Not mad at all."

He lightly brushed his lips over hers. Then he settled his mouth more firmly against hers. Slowly he skimmed his tongue along the outer edge before circling back to create a figure eight like he'd seen a trick roper do once.

She sighed as she looped her arms around his back. He urged her to part her lips, and when she complied, he eased his tongue into the welcoming abyss. Heat roared through him like a prairie fire left unattended. He deepened the kiss, and her embrace tightened as she released a tiny whimper.

Breathing harshly, as though he'd been running after a stampeding herd, he trailed his mouth along the ivory column of her throat. "Ah, Sam, I'm so glad you're not a boy," he croaked in a voice that he barely recognized as his own.

"Me, too."

Lifting his head, he grinned at her. Her lips were swollen, her face flushed. He combed his fingers through her curls.

"I sure know that I'm not looking at a boy now."

His mouth swept down to blanket hers. He kissed her deeply, hungrily, as though he were a starving man offered a fine feast.

Drawing back, he kissed the edge of her chin, the tip of her nose, her brow. "You're still my responsibility, though. Get some sleep."

"What are you going to do?" she asked.

"Keep watch."

"Wake me when it's my turn."

He bussed a quick kiss over her lips. "All right."

He watched as she settled into sleep, curled on her side, her hand tucked beneath her cheek. He was determined that her turn wouldn't come until dawn.

CHAPTER EIGHTEEN

The first rays of the morning sun danced across Sam's eyelids. With a yawn and a leisurely stretch, she opened her eyes.

Matt lay beside her, his hand clasped around hers. He'd never awakened her for a watch. She wondered when he'd succumbed to sleep. He looked peaceful, the lines in his face not quite as deep as usual.

With a smile, she remembered the kiss he'd given her. And the promise not to reveal her secret to Jake. This morning, she thought the sun shone more brightly and the wind blew more gently. Everything was going to be all right.

She eased her hand out of his. She stood and walked down to the river. Kneeling at the water's edge, she washed the sleep from her eyes. Then she sat back on her heels.

Swimming in a river with no cattle milling in it wasn't frightening. She just had to remember that what had happened at the Red River might never happen again.

And if it did, she'd be more prepared.

Out of the corner of her eye, she watched as Matt walked toward her. Taking her hand, he pulled her to her feet, then drew her into his arms.

Eagerly, she welcomed his kiss. Her knees grew weak and her toes curled as she wound her arms around his neck. Warmth sluiced through her, chasing away any early morning chill that lingered.

He broke off the kiss and leaned back. "I'm gonna miss that when we get back to the herd."

His smoldering gaze made her stomach quiver. "Me, too," she admitted.

Crouched at the edge of the group of cowboys gathered around Sam, Matt had an incredible urge to kiss those lips that were spouting the words to Charles Dickens' *A Tale of Two Cities*. The other fellas were engrossed with the book that Cookie had pulled out of the wagon and handed off to Sam to read. Matt figured they'd be a sight more absorbed with the reading if they realized they were listening to a girl.

He still couldn't get over the fact that no one seemed to notice how delicate Sam looked. Of course, she tended to allow a layer of dust to coat her face. But he knew below that dust was a smattering of freckles that dotted her nose and cheeks.

It was pure torment to ride beside her each day, every night, and not be able to hold her, kiss her, or just touch her. Even sleeping next to her was torture. Her gentle breathing was like a lullaby, lulling him into sleep. But throughout the night, he'd awaken with a start, afraid that he was going to find himself folded around her. Afraid he might do for real what he did in his dreams—hold her close and kiss her like there was no tomorrow.

He shifted his gaze slightly as Jake sat beside him.

"You and Sam seem to have mended whatever fences you'd broken," Jake said in a low voice, as though he knew the men wouldn't forgive him for disturbing Sam while she read.

"Going on that scouting mission sure helped," he admitted, grinning inwardly with the memory of how much he'd enjoyed being with her away from everyone else. "You need any more scouting done, you just let us know."

"I prefer to do the scouting myself. I've been hearing tales that the farmers in Kansas are loading up their rifles and trying to stop the cattle from coming through," Jake murmured.

Matt felt anxiety reel through him. Longhorn cattle tended to carry tick fever. They never came down sick, but the livestock that came into contact with them did. Kansas and Missouri had passed quarantine laws prohibiting cattle from coming through during the summer months when the ticks were active. But they'd be loco to try and herd cattle in winter. "What are we going to do?"

Jake shrugged. "We'll see what happens." He slapped Matt's back. "We'll hit the river tomorrow."

Matt nodded. It took a lot longer to move a herd of

cattle than it did to travel on horseback. And it was a lot harder to prod cattle across a river than it was to ride a horse through it. This time, he'd make dadgum certain that Sam stayed by his side.

The river that had looked so peaceful three days earlier now churned up the brown water with the cattle's passing. Even riding drag was no guarantee that trouble wasn't waiting to happen.

Matt glanced over at Sam. She was staring at the water with her brow furrowed and her green eyes darkening. Her bandanna hung loosely around her neck. The corners of that luscious mouth of hers were turned down.

"You gonna be all right?" he asked.

She turned her head slightly and gave him a tremulous smile. "Yeah."

But she looked pale, and sweat beaded above her upper lip. This river was the first they'd had to cross with cattle since she'd nearly drowned and he'd discovered she was a girl. "You want to ride with me?" he asked.

She shook her head slightly and thrust up her chin. "Nope. I'm a trail hand, and hands guide the cattle across the river."

His respect for her grew. She had true grit, that was for sure. He desperately wanted to reach across and squeeze her hand or plant a kiss on that tempting mouth of hers. "I won't let you drown, Samantha Jane."

"One of these days, Matthew Hart, I'm going to come to your rescue." She released a bravado yell and urged her horse down the steep bank and into the deep river.

Matt followed, wondering if she hadn't already come to his aid, rescuing his heart from a self-imposed exile.

During the war, it had hurt to see so many wounded, killed, or taken prisoner. He'd thought it was best not to care . . . and then he'd spotted Sam.

Although he tried not to, he did care. He cared for Sam a lot.

CHAPTER NINETEEN

Long after they'd crossed the river, as night began to wrap itself around her, Sam finally felt the tension easing away as she sat near the campfire. She hadn't been frightened crossing the river, just cautious. Apprehensive. A little concerned that she'd topple off her horse.

But the crossing had gone well. No mishaps at all. Which Jake announced was rare, indeed.

What she couldn't understand was the reason that everyone seemed to be so incredibly wary, as though they didn't quite trust their good fortune. As though at any minute hell would be unleashed.

She studied the cards she held in her hands. Her mother would never approve of her playing poker, but the boredom that twisted its way among the men was as dangerous as any wild steer. She'd seen fights break out simply because one man's shadow had touched another's.

She welcomed any form of entertainment, and if she was very careful, she might not lose much of her earnings. She intended to be very cautious.

"It's too durn quiet," Squirrel said in a low voice, as though he feared disturbing the silence.

"It ain't the quiet," Slim whispered. "It's the stillness."

She expected someone to laugh or make a wisecrack about them worrying like little old maids. Instead, Jed and Jeb just nodded. Even Matt seemed on edge.

"Are you playin' or jawin'?" Sam asked, feigning irritation. The night air did somehow seem different. Thick, almost—oppressive. An air of foreboding loomed over them.

"I'm out," Matt said, tossing down his cards.

Each fella in turn did the same. Sam gathered up her winnings. All twelve pennies. "What are you fellas fretting over?"

"Stampede," Matt said, holding her gaze.

"Why borrow trouble?" Sam asked.

"Ain't borrowing it," Matt said. "Just want to be ready for it."

"How do you get ready for it?" Sam asked.

His gaze dipped to her lips before he abruptly unfolded his body and stood. "Take a walk with me, Sam, and I'll explain it."

She set the cards aside and rose to her feet. As he started walking away from camp, she fell into step beside him. The land was hauntingly barren. No trees to speak of. Just miles of prairie grasses.

They walked until they could no longer hear Cookie rattling pans or the murmuring of cowboys. The campfire was far behind them. Beside her, Matt was only a silhouette. Yet she could feel his intense gaze smoldering as it traveled over her.

"Thought you were going to explain things," she said quietly.

"Yep." He stopped walking and faced her. "I have a powerful urge to kiss you, Samantha Jane."

Pleasure tingled through her from her head to her toes. She heard his sigh float on the gentle breeze.

"But someone with good eyes might see what I was doing—"

"And figure out that I wasn't a boy," she finished for him.

"Yep."

A corner of her mouth curled up. "Is that what you wanted to explain to me?"

"I just wanted to be alone with you for a bit. I've never done any real courting. Not sure how to go about it properly."

Her heart thudded against her chest. "Are you saying you want to court me?"

"I'm saying I'm thinking about it."

She certainly hadn't come on this drive expecting to find a beau, and she wasn't entirely sure that she had. "Matt, have you ever looked through a window into a store and seen something that you wanted but couldn't have?"

"Sure."

"And the fact that you couldn't have it makes you

want it that much more."

"What are you getting at?" he asked.

"I'm just wondering if you're wanting to kiss me or court me because you can't," she said softly. "I'm like forbidden fruit. Tempting because you can't have me."

"You think if I could kiss you, then I wouldn't want you anymore?" Matt asked.

The words sounded so silly to Sam coming out of his mouth. "I don't know."

"Then let's find out." He pulled her to him.

"Matt! Someone might see—"

His mouth cut off her protest as effectively as a tornado ended a Sunday picnic. He kissed her, slowly, provocatively. She actually imagined she could hear a fiddle humming, but it was just the blood thrumming between her temples. Threading his fingers through her hair, he angled her head slightly and deepened the kiss.

She heard his guttural groan and answered with a moan of her own.

Breathing harshly, he pulled back and released her. He backed up a step. "So much for your theory. I want you more now than I did a minute ago." He spun on his heel.

"Where are you going?" she asked.

"To check on the cattle and get my mind off you."

She watched his retreating shadow until he blended in with the night and disappeared. A burst of distant lightning briefly illuminated the sky, outlining him.

With his head bent, he cut such a lonesome figure. And she wondered if he'd realized what she finally understood.

Whenever he kissed her, a tiny spark of passion ignited into a flame. A flame that could be as dangerous as a brush fire burning across the prairie, destroying all in its path.

She had to stay clear of him. If she didn't rein in the passion smoldering between them, it could destroy all her dreams.

Startled awake, Sam felt the thunder long before she heard it. The ground rumbled beneath her, trembling as though it feared at any moment it would crack open and swallow up everything that surrounded it.

"Stampede!" someone yelled.

She sat bolt upright. Beside her, Matt had already pulled on his boots.

"You stay here," he threw over his shoulder as he took off at a run.

Everyone was scrambling around the camp; those who had removed their britches before going to sleep weren't bothering to put them on now. They were content to run around in their long drawers.

Sam was certain that Matt's order had meant he was getting her horse ready. She pulled on her boots and rushed to the remuda, where cowboys were quickly saddling their horses. She reached for the rope keeping

Cinnamon tethered to the line.

Matt grabbed her arm and pulled her back. "I told you to stay put!"

She wrenched free. "There's a stampede. I can get my horse ready."

"You're not riding. You stay by the wagon with Cookie."

Her mouth agape, she stared at him. "What? Matt, you need every rider—"

"What I *need* is not to have to worry about *you!*"

"I can handle myself," she assured him.

He shook his head forcefully. "Not during a stampede."

"What's going on here?" Jake asked, his face a mask of concern, irritation, and dread.

"Sam's staying," Matt told him.

"No, I'm not."

"I don't have time to argue, Sam," Matt said. "You're staying."

"He's going," Jake said.

Matt jerked his gaze to Jake. "Sam has no experience handling stampeding cattle."

"Then he'll get it tonight. Mount up." He spun on his heel.

"Sam's a girl!" Matt yelled.

Sam felt her dreams come crashing around her as everyone stilled, mouths unhinged, eyes wide.

Jake twisted around so quickly that he almost lost his

balance. "What did you say?"

Matt took a deep breath. "I said that Sam is a girl."

Jake swore harshly beneath his breath. "Cookie, keep her at the wagon." He pointed a trembling finger at Matt. "I'll deal with you later."

He stormed away.

She pounded her fist into Matt's shoulder. "You betrayed me. You promised—"

"We'll discuss it after we get the cattle calmed," he said reaching for his horse.

"I'll hate you until the day I die!" she yelled as he mounted up.

He looked down on her. "At least I don't have to worry about your dying tonight."

He twirled his horse about and galloped off into the night.

And all Sam felt was the destruction of her dreams and the shattering of her heart.

CHAPTER TWENTY

Sitting on the ground with her back against a wagon wheel, Sam watched the storm rolling across the land. Flashing sheets of lightning followed by resonant thunder. Although there was no rain, the air felt charged with expectation.

She could certainly understand why the cattle had decided to stampede tonight. She desperately wanted to run herself. She'd worked until her fingers were raw, every muscle and bone in her body ached. She'd faced the river.

And for what?

For betrayal. She'd earned the right to be respected, to be thought capable of handling a stampeding herd. Instead, she'd been relinquished to waiting and worrying and wondering.

Beneath her backside, the ground still trembled with the pounding of hooves.

"Eerie, ain't it?" Cookie asked as he put another coffee pot on the stones he carried with him to place around the fire.

She glanced over at him. He was wiping his hands on his apron.

"Cattle don't make a dadgum sound except for the thundering of their hooves. I think the dang silence bothers me most," he said.

For some inexplicable reason, she shivered. "I don't know why I had to stay behind."

"So you'd be safe."

"I didn't think any place was safe during a stampede," she muttered. She knew she should be grateful that Matt cared, but it angered her that he didn't trust her to do the job.

"A wagon is usually safe. I don't know why, but cattle won't trample over a wagon. If they start heading this way, you just get on the other side of it. They'll go around. No matter how many steers there are, no matter how fast they're going." He chuckled. "I've stood with my quaking back against the wagon and watched 'em rush by like the parted waters."

Sitting here, wondering what was going on out there on the prairie, was driving her crazy. She scrambled to her feet. "What can I do to help?"

He grinned. "That's the fighting spirit, gal. Let's get some water to boiling. Probably have to clean some scrapes and cuts. And the men will want lots of coffee. Once cattle get it into their heads to stampede, they're hard to settle down. Doesn't take much to set them to running again."

She grabbed a pot off his well-organized wagon and

began to ladle water into it from the water barrel. "Have you seen many stampedes, Cookie?"

"Yep. Before the war, I worked for men herding the cattle to California. During the war, worked for outfits trying to get beef to the Confederacy." He swung his arm in an arch. "Now, I got this."

She set the pot on a hooked pole that Cookie had stabbed into the earth. "Have you ever seen a woman on a cattle drive?"

"Not until this one." He squinted at her. "What were you thinking, gal?"

"That a hundred dollars would ease my ma's burden."

He shook his head. "How long has Matt known?"

She licked her lips, trying to decide whether she should answer. What could it hurt? "Since we crossed the Red."

Cookie swore harshly. Then his cheeks turned red. "Beggin' your pardon. Jake is gonna skin that boy alive and hang him up to dry."

Good. He deserved it. Not for keeping her secret, but for revealing it.

She heard galloping horses and turned to see some trail hands switch out their mounts for fresh horses. She ran over to them. "How's it going?"

"They're scattered to the four winds," Squirrel said.

"Maybe I ought to ride with you and help," she suggested.

"I'd rather you didn't," Slim said. "Jake would cut us

loose quicker than you could blink."

Disappointed, she nodded.

Squirrel mounted his horse. "For what it's worth, I thought you were a fair hand—for a first-timer."

She smiled as he kicked his horse into a gallop. "Be careful!"

Turning away, she headed back toward the camp to see what else she could do to help Cookie. She thought she'd been a fair hand as well.

Hell on hooves.

That's all Matt could think as he galloped over the prairie, trying to get in front of the lead steer. A man didn't want to fall from his horse and get caught beneath all those hooves.

Matt had heard tales of men being pounded into the ground until all that was visible was their hat. Probably nothing more than a tall Texas tale. But he had no plans to test whether it was legend or fact.

The men were as silent as the cattle. The cattle didn't bawl and the men didn't yell. No need to spook the critters any more than they were already spooked. Besides, the men knew what to do without speaking.

The hands needed to get the cattle to start turning in on themselves, to form a circle that the men could gradually guide the cattle into—smaller and smaller, until they had no choice but to stop running. And once they were settled, they'd still be jittery and nervous.

The least little sound would start them off again.

A group of cattle detoured from the main herd. Matt swore under his breath. Once they started splitting up, it made it harder to get them back in line. A man had to stay on the outside and not get caught in the middle.

Even if Sam hadn't been a girl, Matt would have argued with Jake about letting her ride tonight. A haunting stillness hung heavy in the air. It made the hairs on the back of his neck prickle with unease.

Sam. He understood that she was madder than a hornet trapped in a bonnet. He didn't even blame her. He had betrayed her, but in his mind he'd had no choice. He didn't have time to argue with her or convince her of the merits of staying behind.

With her out here, they would both have been at risk, because he would have had his mind on her, on trying to protect her. If the sacrifice was the loss of her affection, so be it. He'd rather have her hate than have her dead.

He urged his horse into a faster gallop as the cattle once again veered off. He felt rain splatter on his hat. Good. If the rain came, maybe the storm would pass.

An electric storm was the worse. He watched lightning streak across the sky and dance over horns. It was a frightening sight.

The gully appeared out of nowhere. He heard the cattle bawling as they plunged over its edge.

He heard his horse's high-squealing neigh. It pitched forward into the abyss. Matt leaped free of the chaos. But in the darkness, he couldn't see. He could only feel the agonizing pain ripping through him.

Before the merciful peace of oblivion claimed him.

Something was wrong; Sam felt it clear down to her bones as the rain began to fall in torrents. Matt wasn't a coward. Neither was he a fool.

He had to know that his horse couldn't keep at a gallop all night. He had to understand that facing Sam's wrath was preferable to wearing his horse down to nothing. Besides, she didn't think he'd slink away from confronting her.

He'd meet her head on. He no doubt expected them to have words as soon as the cattle were quieted.

So why hadn't he returned to camp to get a fresh horse?

The other men had, some more than once. They gulped down the cups of coffee she offered them, then leaped onto their horses and rode back into the night with only a few words spoken.

"They must have run a good fifteen to twenty miles."

"Had 'em calmed for a while, then they just took off like someone poked 'em."

"Figure we've probably lost a hundred."

"Some didn't have the sense to get out of the way. I keep running across trampled carcasses."

It was the last comment tossed onto the wind that

bothered her the most. She figured two thousand head at a dead run could do a lot of damage. Even though Cookie continued to reassure her that cattle wouldn't cut across the wagon, it didn't mean they wouldn't trample a man and his horse.

"Need help here!" someone yelled. "Jeb is hurt!"

Sam snapped out of her reverie. Jed was pulling back on the reins, drawing his horse to a halt. Jeb was sitting behind his brother. With a grunt he slid off the back end of the horse.

His hat was gone, his clothing was muddy, and his arm was dangling at his side like a scarecrow's in a corn field.

Jed dismounted and led his brother toward the fire. "Jeb fell from his horse."

"Dang it, boy," Cookie muttered as he lumbered over.

Jeb dropped onto the ground and cradled one arm in his lap. Sam knelt beside him. "Is it broken?" she asked.

Nodding, he rolled back his sleeve. Sam's stomach roiled at the sight of the bone pushing against the flesh.

"Head back out," Cookie ordered Jed. "Me and Sam can tend this."

Jed nodded and then he was gone.

Sam held Jeb's hand and wiped his brow while Cookie set the broken bone into place.

"How did you fall?" Sam asked quietly, trying to distract Jeb from the pain.

"Horse dropped his leg into a prairie-dog hole. Jed had

to put him down. Broke his leg. Broke my arm."

"Does that happen often, men getting this badly hurt?" Sam asked.

"Not unusual to lose a man or two when the cattle are as riled up as they are tonight. I knew it was a spooky night. I could feel it in the air," Jeb said.

"Did you see Matt while you were out there?" she asked.

He shook his head. "Cattle are spread out everywhere, though. We're all just doing the best we can."

She glanced over at the splint that Cookie had finished putting together.

"Reckon we can expect injuries to start coming in now," he mumbled.

And he was right. Sam served up coffee and tender ministrations. She applied a damp cloth to a huge lump on one man's head. Men limped around the camp. More men began to filter into camp, reporting that the cattle were spread out but calmed.

Some men fell flat onto their pallets and immediately began to snore. Others drank the coffee and ate the sourdough biscuits she offered right before they headed back out. But Matt never returned to camp.

The sunrise was just a sliver along the horizon, beginning to push aside the night. She tromped over to the remaining horses and began to saddle Cinnamon.

"What are you doing?" Squirrel asked.

"Something's wrong. Matt hasn't returned to camp," she told him.

"A lot of fellas are staying out there," Squirrel said.

How could she explain this feeling of dread that had been creeping over her? "But they've returned to camp off and on. Even Jake has returned to camp." Not as often as some of the men, but he had come back at least twice that she'd seen.

"I'll go with you," Squirrel said.

She didn't know whether to draw comfort from his presence or worry because he had thought, just as she did, that there was a need to go in search of Matt.

CHAPTER TWENTY-ONE

The torrential rain eased off into an irritating drizzle. The drops fell from the brim of Sam's hat. That her face and shoulders were protected offered her little comfort. Like most of the cowboys, she'd slipped on her poncho when she'd felt the first bit of moisture hit.

So beneath the poncho she was drier than an empty well. Still she was miserable. She couldn't shake off this dreadful sense of foreboding.

As the sun began to ease higher, she could see the cattle clustered in small groups.

Before her spread an expanse of land that was as breathtaking as it was daunting. Matt could be anywhere out here. Anywhere at all.

She had no idea where to begin looking . . . until she saw the vultures circling overhead.

Slowly, painstakingly, Matt crawled his way up the side of the gully. He had to get back to camp, had to make sure that Sam was all right. His horse was dead, as were most of the cattle that had plunged headlong into the abyss.

Through the haze of pain, he could hear some bawling.

He wanted to help them, he truly did. But he wasn't even certain that he could help himself. His leg ached like a son-of-a-gun and blood soaked his britches. A protruding horn must have ripped through his thigh.

He shuddered at the memory of the agonizing pain. It was all he remembered. That, and the blackness. And the paralyzing fear.

Breathing harshly, he collapsed at the top of the gully. How much blood had he lost? How long had he been lying there, unconscious? Was Sam all right?

Sam. Her name was a sweet benediction echoing through his mind. He had to get to her. Somehow, he knew that if he could just make his way to her, he'd be all right.

With trembling hands, he worked the knot on his bandanna loose and slid it away from his neck. He wrapped it around his thigh. He needed to make a tourniquet. But he was incredibly weak.

The darkness kept fading in and out. Which made no sense. It appeared to be day.

The earth and sky tilted and swirled.

Thirsty, he was incredibly thirsty. Was his canteen in the gully, still strapped to his saddle horn? Was it wedged beneath his horse and the cattle? Would he have the strength to retrieve it if he tried?

The questions, the doubts, pounded at him unmercifully. He couldn't think clearly. He seemed capable only of worrying about Sam. What would happen to her if Matt couldn't get back to camp?

He heard thunder. Beneath his cheek that was pressed to the dirt, the ground shook. *Not another stampede. Please, not another stampede.*

He didn't think he'd have any luck getting out of the way this time. He'd lost his hat. No one would know where he'd been trampled.

"Oh, Matt!"

Raising his throbbing head, he squinted through the sweat and dirt. *Sam!* A corner of his mouth quirked up. "You sure are a sight for sore eyes."

"What happened?" she asked as she dropped down beside him.

"Bad luck."

Sam thought it was more than bad luck as she lifted Matt's head and tilted a tin cup against his mouth. She'd helped Squirrel get Matt onto Squirrel's horse so they could get him back to camp. The journey had been slow and arduous, with Matt gritting his teeth the entire trek.

He'd groaned only once—and that was when Squirrel had put him on the horse. She wished he wouldn't remain so stoic. It made it difficult for her to remain angry with him.

It made it even harder to remain angry when she'd been

so dadgum relieved to see him alive.

Now he lay on a pallet, breathing harshly through clenched teeth. The trail hands had surrounded him as though they'd never seen an injured man before.

Sam sat beside him. He had his hand clutched around hers. It felt clammy and cold. Unnatural sweat beaded his brow and his upper lip.

Cookie cut the leg of Matt's bloodied britches, pulling the cloth aside, and exposing the dastardly gash in his thigh. Sam darted a quick glance at his wound. It looked as though a steer had torn unmercifully into it. She could only imagine that the cow had been mad with fright, and Matt had been caught in the madness.

"Gawd Almighty," Cookie breathed.

"That bad, huh?" Matt asked, his gaze never wavering from Sam's face as though she was his tether in the storm. She couldn't blame him for not wanting to see.

"It's gotta be stitched," Cookie announced, as though no one else could draw the same conclusion.

"I'll do it," Sam said quietly. She'd seen Cookie treat the others. The man might be skilled with healing, and the cowboys might all acknowledge that he was the camp doctor, but he wasn't gentle. She couldn't bear the thought of Matt being in any more pain that he already was.

She heard the clanking of spurs. The men gathered around quickly parted and Jake knelt beside Matt.

"What happened?" he asked.

"Didn't see the gully," Matt said. "Cattle were frantic. Sam found me."

Jake jerked his attention to her. "You went searching for him?"

She wasn't certain if the disbelief in his voice was because she'd disobeyed his order to stay at camp or because she'd had the gumption not to wait.

"He didn't come back to camp, not once," she explained. "Everyone else came back for coffee or to switch horses. You were long gone by the time I started to get concerned. I was afraid to wait until you came back to go searching for him in case he was in trouble."

"Which I was," Matt said.

"Reckon he's lucky you didn't wait then," Jake said, and she almost thought she heard admiration in his voice.

"We need to get this mess in his leg taken care of, Boss," Cookie said.

"All right. It's gonna take us most of the day to round up the cattle. Do what you can for Matt. I'll check back at nightfall." He stood up and strode away.

Cookie set a bowl of warm water in front of Sam. She quickly washed her hands.

"Bite down on this," Cookie ordered and Sam watched as he slid a strip of leather between Matt's teeth. Then he poured whiskey over the wound.

Slamming his eyes closed, Matt jerked and hissed through his teeth. Tears burned Sam's eyes. She wanted to stay angry with him for betraying her, but all she seemed capable of doing was wishing that his torment would be over.

Looking away from Matt, she slipped sturdy black thread through a large needle. Then, with a shuddering breath, she steeled herself for what she had to do. And went to work.

The fever hit Matt hard in the middle of the night. It had been hovering most of the day. Every time Sam had run a damp cloth over his brow or along his throat, she had felt it just below his skin, the warmth that ran more deeply than body heat.

She'd fed him broth throughout the day and given him plenty of water to drink. She'd sponged him off, over and over, trying to keep him cool. She'd changed his dressing more often than was probably needed, but she worried about infection setting in. She didn't want him to lose his leg. Even more, she didn't want him to die.

One by one, the men would come over to check on him. Shifting from foot to foot, hands tucked behind the waistband of their britches, they all seemed uncomfortable with Matt's discomfort as though they'd somehow failed him by not noticing that he was missing.

"How's he doing?" Jake asked as he squatted beside her.

"He's fevered," Sam said quietly.

"That's not unusual out here. Infection can set in quick. Or his body could just be fighting. But he's strong and stubborn. We'll hole up here as long as we have to." He twisted slightly and looked at her. "I can't believe Matt hired a girl."

"He didn't know that I was a girl at the time," she admitted.

"But he figured it out."

She nodded. "At the Red River."

He heaved a sigh. "He should have told me that day."

"He wanted to, but I talked him out of it," she said hastily. She was willing to shoulder the responsibility for the entire fiasco.

"Don't you have family?" Jake asked.

"Of course I do. Why do you think I'm doing this? We needed the money. We still do."

"The next town is Baxter Springs. You'll be leaving us there."

She considered arguing, begging him to let her stay, but she didn't think the time was right. He was weary; she could see it in his eyes. He'd battled cattle all night and day. Maybe if she waited until his mood improved . . . but she couldn't recall ever seeing him in an improved mood.

"I'll be out with the cattle. Send someone to fetch me

if Matt's fever gets worse." With that final command, he stood and strode away.

She tried not to think about how she'd be leaving the outfit once they got to the next town. It was just a hop, skip, and a jump from Baxter Springs to Sedalia. But if she didn't make it to Sedalia with the outfit, she wouldn't get her hundred dollars. It didn't matter how far she'd come or how hard she'd worked.

She'd be left with nothing but broken dreams.

But at least she wasn't broken physically, as Matt was. She dipped the cloth into the bowl of water. Lifting it, she wrung it out and tenderly began to wipe away the sweat that coated Matt's chest. Cookie had removed Matt's shirt shortly after Sam had finished tending the wound on his thigh. He'd wanted to check his ribs.

Matt's ribs were all intact, but it was obvious from the dark shadows forming on his skin that he'd been battered by stampeding cattle in the gully. One side was almost completely black and blue. The rest of him was a series of bruises.

She hated the thought of him caught in that gully. She might have been able to do something if they'd been riding together. She wouldn't have left his side as the others had.

She knew her thoughts were unfair. No one had intentionally abandoned him. They were all just doing what they could to calm the herd and get them back in line.

Slowly she trailed the cloth along his throat, over his broad shoulders, and across his chest. His muscles were taut from hard work. Gingerly, she moved the cloth over his ribs down to his flat stomach. Back up again to his throat. Back down. A wide circle. Then a smaller one.

"I had to tell Jake, Sam," Matt rasped.

Snapping her gaze up to his, she wondered how long he'd been awake, how long he might have been watching her.

"Don't you see?" he continued. "It could have been you lying here."

Tears welled in her eyes. "I wish it was. Don't die on me, Matt."

A corner of his mouth quirked up. "Wouldn't dream of it . . . but I sure am dreaming of this . . ."

He plowed his fingers through her hair and curled his hand around the back of her head. He urged her closer, closer, until their mouths touched.

The kiss was filled with desperation as though he needed to affirm that they were both still alive. Had survived.

When he'd finished kissing her soundly, he guided her face to the nook of his shoulder. "Sleep," he ordered in a weary voice.

"I need to watch you," she murmured.

"Later," was all he said before he drifted off.

His breathing grew even and his skin felt less heated. She gave into temptation and joined him in sleep.

CHAPTER TWENTY-TWO

"Do you have any idea what kind of danger you put this outfit in when you brought her on?" Jake asked.

Matt had hoped that Jake would wait until he was fully recovered to give him a tongue-lashing. Instead he'd only waited until Matt was strong enough to walk on his own.

"I can't see that I put anyone in danger at all," Matt said evenly.

"She's a girl!"

"Who pulls her weight."

"She's leaving the drive at the next town," Jake said, punctuating each word with a jab of his finger in the air.

"We're not that far from Sedalia. Let her stay."

Jake began pacing. "The hardest part is ahead. Getting these cattle by angry Kansas ranchers." He came to an abrupt halt. "How are you going to feel if she takes a bullet?"

As though the lead had torn into his own heart. Matt plowed his hands through his hair. These cattle were his family's legacy, a chance to rebuild after the war. He had to put them first. But he couldn't stand the thought of disappointing Sam. "Go ahead and pay her the full salary at the next town."

"If I do that, then every man in this outfit will expect the same treatment and they'll head out. Why face the dangers if the trail boss is willing to hand out money early? *Then* who will drive the cattle to market?" Jake asked.

"There has to be a way—"

"She never should have joined up! And as long as I'm the trail boss, as long as I run the outfit, women can sit at home and wait for us to return to them. At the next town, Matt, she's parting company with us, one way or another. She goes or I do."

Matt didn't have the experience to run the outfit. If only the hardest part were behind them, he thought he could manage it. But Jake was right: they'd come so far, but they still had a ways to go, and they needed a man leading them who knew not only the terrain, but cattle and men.

He slowly nodded his acceptance of the wisdom of Jake's words.

Now Jake poked his finger against Matt's chest. "And you not only get to break the news to her, but make arrangements for her to go home. And that little expense can come out of your pocket."

Matt watched him storm away. He should have known it would be impossible to reason with Jake. The stampede had cost them close to two hundred head, and Matt's injury had put them further behind schedule.

With a heavy heart, he limped gingerly across the camp to where Sam stood beside her horse.

"He said I have to go," she blurted out.

"Yeah. At the next town."

She nodded jerkily. He could see her chin quivering.

"He's just repeating what you've been saying ever since you found out I was a girl," she said.

"It's for the best, Sam."

"Is it, Matt?" she asked. Her gaze dipped to his leg. "Maybe it is, at that."

She mounted her horse. "Now that everyone knows I'm a girl, I don't see that you have to shadow my moves anymore. I'll be fine until we get to Baxter Springs."

He watched her horse canter toward the herd, taking a piece of his heart with her.

They were making camp for the night about twenty miles from Baxter Springs. Matt stood at the edge of the camp, near the supply wagon. The mood among the men was somber.

They all knew what he'd be doing tomorrow. Taking Sam to town and making arrangements for her to get back to Texas with some sort of escort.

It came as no surprise to him that his chore didn't sit well with most of the men. It didn't sit well with him, either.

During the war, he'd followed orders even when he

didn't agree with them. He'd marched into battle when he knew the odds were against them winning.

He'd had no say in how they fought or when they fought or where they fought. He'd lost everyone who'd ever mattered to him. Lost everyone of importance, until he'd stopped letting anyone matter.

He'd built a wall of ice around his heart, a cold shell behind which he could retreat. It was easier to dig graves for those he barely knew, easier to listen to the cries of men whose names he didn't recognize.

He'd become hard and callous because it was the only way he thought he could survive. No one mattered.

Until Sam. Sam mattered.

Sam mattered so much that it hurt to see her moping around the camp. It was agony to watch her putting on a show of indifference as she went about whatever meaningless tasks Jake gave her.

But no matter where she was or what she was doing, she haunted Matt.

He was letting her down. Just like he'd disappointed the boys under his command—before he'd become uncaring.

She'd forged ahead and looked for him when it would have been safer to stay behind. She was accepting Jake's sentence of a trip to Baxter Springs because she was one girl against a passel of cowboys.

One girl . . . with whom he'd fallen in love.

* * *

Sitting beside the fire, Sam knew that come daylight, her time as a trail hand would end. She didn't want to think about all she had sacrificed, all she was going to give up.

She didn't want to contemplate how disappointed her family would be when she returned empty-handed. Or how disappointed she would be to return with nothing to show for all her hard work.

She hadn't spoken a word to Matt since the morning when he'd told her about Jake's decision. She knew she shouldn't blame him . . . but if he'd only kept his dang mouth shut, hadn't tried to protect her, she might have had a chance to pull off this deception.

As it was, she had nothing.

Matt continued to ride drag, but Jake had moved her up to point. Not as a reward, but as a punishment. To have her closer, so he could keep an eye on her.

Matt no longer set up his pallet near hers. They no longer shared the night watch. He always found someone to trade with him.

She was grateful; she truly was. But she was also disappointed. Sometimes, she didn't know how she felt about Matt. She longed to talk with him, but it hurt to think of him betraying her.

She glanced up as Jake brought his horse to a halt near the supply wagon. He looked extremely unhappy as he dismounted and strode into the middle of camp.

"Listen up!" he yelled, and all the men moved in closer.

Sam expected that he was going to announce that they had to draw names to determine who was to escort her to town. But she quickly realized his expression was too grave for such an insignificant matter as her trip to town.

"The Kansas farmers are in an uproar over this tick fever that some longhorn cattle carry. Rumors are that they're going to get their rifles and try to stop any cattle crossing into Kansas or Missouri," Jake said.

Sam glanced around at the men. They were furrowing their brows and tightening their lips into straight lines. Her gaze clashed with Matt's, and she wondered what he was thinking. Was he remembering their kisses, the closeness they'd felt by the river?

"What exactly does that mean, Boss?" Slim asked.

"We've got to move and move fast if we want to get our cattle to Sedalia before these farmers are completely organized and cut off the routes," he said.

"Sounds like you're gonna need every man to work harder than he has been," Matt said.

"That's right," Jake agreed. "We'll leave an hour earlier in the morning, ride two hours later into the evening."

"You're gonna need every trail hand you have," Matt said quietly.

A hush fell over the men, and Sam's heart kicked up. She thought she could have heard a leaf landing on the ground as Matt and Jake stared at each other.

Jake finally nodded. "You're right once again. I will. You'll need to hightail it back here as fast as you can once you take Sam to Baxter Springs tomorrow."

Matt shifted his gaze to her. His eyes held a sadness that she didn't know how to interpret. He turned his attention back to Jake.

"I'm not taking Sam to Baxter Springs."

"You're the one who hired her. You're the one who gets to escort her out of here."

"I hired her and I'm damned glad that I did. She's a first-rate trail hand, Jake, and you know it," Matt said. "She's never shirked her responsibilities to us, even when we've shrugged off ours to her. She's crossed rivers when she was terrified, fought prairie fires when she knew it was safer to stay behind—when she was *ordered* to stay behind. She's tended our wounds, and continued to help out even when she knows she won't be paid."

Sam's chest tightened with his announcement, and more, with the realization that he was acknowledging the work she'd done for the outfit.

Jake shook his head. "I'm aware of everything she's done. But the dangers of armed farmers and moving the cattle fast is too much of a risk for her and for us. I'm not willing to risk having a girl in the outfit."

"Then I reckon you won't have me either," Matt said quietly.

Sam was on the verge of protesting when someone said, "Or me."

"Or me," Slim said.

"Or me," Squirrel announced.

"Or me," Jeb and Jed said at the same time.

One by one, the other cowboys voiced their support of her, each stepping back until Jake stood alone in the center of the camp.

Jake swept his hat from his head. "Look, fellas, I appreciate how you all feel about Sam, but if you leave now, you won't get paid."

"I reckon I'm not getting paid, either," Cookie said, "since I'll be leaving as well."

In her short stint as a trail hand, Sam had learned that the one man almost as important as the trail boss—and some would argue, more important—was the cook.

Tears stung her eyes as she thought of all they were willing to give up for her. "You fellas don't have to do this for me."

"Why not, Sam? Wouldn't you do the same for one of us?" Matt asked.

Of course she would, and he knew it.

She met and held Jake's gaze. "You told me never to lie to you again, so I'm going to tell you the honest-to-gosh truth. If I didn't think I could contribute to the outfit, you wouldn't have to escort me to Baxter Springs. I'd go on my own. But Mr. Vaughn, I honestly believe I can help you get these cattle to Sedalia before the trouble starts."

"I've never had a problem with your work, Sam," Jake said. "If you were a boy—"

"It wouldn't make a difference," she interrupted.

"Maybe you're right," he conceded. "I do know I can't get the cattle moving if I don't have a crew. Since these cowpunchers seem to be as loyal to you as you are to them . . . I reckon you can stay."

The cowboys tossed their hats in the air as their yells echoed around her. Sam blinked back her tears of joy. It wouldn't do for a trail hand to cry.

And that's what they were all acknowledging that she was at long last. A trail hand.

CHAPTER TWENTY-THREE

Faithful, Texas
Six weeks later

Samantha sank into the hot water that lapped against the sides of the wooden tub. The steam tickled her nose and the heat eased the ache in her weary body. She'd arrived home less than an hour ago and immediately doled out her presents.

A new dress for Amy. Broad-brimmed hats for Nate and Benjamin. A locket for her mother.

But the best gift of all had been the note from Mr. Thomas at the general store, saying their debt had been paid in full. With all her purchases, Samantha still had money left over to give to her mother. Money that would help get them through the coming autumn and winter.

It had taken the herd three weeks to get to Sedalia. She'd watched as they'd counted and loaded the cattle onto boxcars. She'd hardly been able to believe that her days as a trail hand had come to an end.

Returning to Faithful had gone much more quickly because their journey hadn't been hampered by the slow-moving steers.

Some of the cowboys had gone their own way after Sedalia, but her favorites had traveled back to Texas: Matt, Slim, Squirrel, Jed, and Jeb. Jake and Cookie had been with them as well, intent on returning to the Broken Heart ranch.

She was having a difficult time believing that she was home. It appeared her mother was as well. With the hem of her apron, she kept wiping the tears from her eyes.

"It shouldn't have been you who had to provide for us," her mother rasped, clutching the pouch that held what was left from the hundred dollars.

Through half-lowered lashes, Samantha peered at her mother. "Ma, I wanted to do it."

"You seem so much older, hardly like my little girl anymore."

"I reckon I grew up some." Using the scented soap she'd purchased from the general store, she began washing the weeks of grime from her body. "It was an adventure, Ma."

"You always did want to go on an adventure," her mother reminded her.

Samantha smiled. "And I'll tell my grandchildren about this one."

Her mother picked up the pile of filthy clothes in the corner. "I think these should be burned."

"I'm looking forward to putting on a dress again. Looking like a girl," Samantha admitted.

"There's a dance in town tonight. I reckon Amy's going to want to wear her new dress," her mother said.

"Reckon I'll wear mine as well."

"I'll leave you to finish getting ready." Her mother pressed a kiss to the top of Samantha's head. "It's so good to have you home again."

After her mother left the room, Samantha leaned her head back against the tub and closed her eyes. She didn't really want to go to the dance. The only fella she wanted to dance with was headed toward his home somewhere south of hers.

Matt had stood up for her outside Baxter Springs. But once she'd been accepted as a true member of the group, he'd treated her more like she was a boy than he had in the days before. Kinda like a younger brother—if he paid any attention to her at all.

He'd never again kissed her. She could only assume the last kiss he'd bestowed upon her had been fever induced. Maybe he'd been delirious. Even after they'd delivered the cattle to Sedalia and she'd held the hundred dollars in her hand, he'd been aloof.

He'd been polite when he'd said good-bye to her that morning, but he'd left her with no promises. Only memories.

Memories of her first trail drive, her first kiss . . . her first love.

With her family in tow, Samantha walked inside the schoolhouse. She'd spotted all the desks outside as Benjamin had pulled their wagon alongside the others. They always used the one-room school for gatherings. On the teacher's raised dais, Mr. Thomas from the general store was tuning his fiddle.

Lanterns hung from walls, casting pale light into the room. She saw her best friend standing in a corner. "Ma, I'm going to go visit with Mary Margaret."

Her mother smiled softly. "Reckon I can let you out of my sight for a little while tonight."

Samantha hurried across the room and threw her arms around Mary Margaret. With a squeal, her friend hugged her tightly.

"You're finally home!" Mary Margaret leaned back. "For pity's sake, Samantha Jane, I can't believe you didn't tell me about this wild scheme of yours."

"There wasn't much time for telling anyone anything." Besides, Samantha had been afraid that somehow the word of her plan would make its way to the trail boss before she'd ever begun the journey. And her cattle days would have come to an abrupt end.

"What was it like being with all those . . . those

men . . . all those weeks?" Mary Margaret asked. She was raised up on her toes as though she expected Samantha's answer to send her into flight.

"It was hard at first," Samantha admitted. "Trying to make sure that they didn't figure out that I wasn't a boy."

"And once they figured it out?"

"They treated me like they had all along—like one of the fellas."

"For pity's sake, Samantha." With a dramatic sigh, Mary Margaret pressed her hand above her breast. "I'm on the verge of swooning at the very thought of you being in the company of men by your lonesome for so long. I want to know all the details."

One day she'd share with Mary Margaret the details regarding Matt, but tonight was too soon. She wanted to savor the memories, hold them close to her heart, and for a while longer, keep them only to herself.

"For the most part, I just trailed along behind the cattle," Samantha said.

"Did the men toss out any profanity?"

"Not that I recall." Oh, they'd grumbled and grouched, but then, so had she from time to time.

"Did they imbibe any alcohol?" Mary Margaret asked eagerly.

"I doubt it. You have to stay alert. A man could get killed if anyone was careless."

"You must have been terrified," Mary Margaret said.

Sam shrugged. "A couple of times. Mostly I was just so grateful to feel useful. To know that I was doing my share, pulling my weight."

"It doesn't sound like any great adventure at all," Mary Margaret said.

Within her heart, though, it had been a wonderful adventure.

Mary Margaret squeezed Samantha's hand. "Can you believe we're having our first dance? I'm so glad you're here to share the night with me. I'm hoping some fella will sweep me right off my feet."

"Maybe Benjamin will ask you to dance."

Mary Margaret slapped her hand at the air. "Oh, I've given up on Benjamin." Suddenly, she grabbed Samantha's arm and jerked her closer. "Oh, my gosh, Samantha. Ain't he a long drink of water?"

Samantha glanced over her shoulder and her heart skipped a beat. No one else but Matt was hovering in the doorway. And Gawd almighty, did he look good. He'd obviously bathed, shaved, and cut his hair. He was wearing clean clothes. No, she realized. They were more than clean—they were brand-spanking new. His boots were polished to a shine.

She thought he was gone, on his way home. What in the world was he doing here?

She knew the moment he spotted her. A slow, lazy smile spread over his face.

"He has to be the most handsome fella I've ever seen," Mary Margaret whispered.

Oh, yes, Samantha thought. He surely was. Her heart thundered against her ribs and her mouth grew dry. With his gaze trained intently on her, he strode confidently across the room until he reached her.

"Hello, Samantha Jane," he said in a slow, sensual drawl.

"I thought you'd gone on." She was surprised to discover that she sounded breathless.

His grin grew. "You know how cowboys are. We wouldn't dream of missing a dance."

Mary Margaret tugged on her arm to gain her attention. She knew her friend wanted an introduction. "Matt, this is my best friend. Mary Margaret."

"Pleasure. There's a few fellas coming through the door behind me who would be right honored to dance with you," he told her.

Mary Margaret's face brightened. "Well, then I'll go introduce myself."

She gave Samantha a speculative look before heading across the room where Slim, Squirrel, Jed, and Jeb were standing near the entrance. Samantha could see them making hasty introductions and she figured Mary Margaret would be dancing all night.

As for her . . . "Matt, what are you doing here?"

"I wanted to see you. To explain why I stayed away from you after the stampede." He rubbed the side of his nose. "Jake told me that if he caught me kissing you or even looking at you like I wanted to . . . he'd take you back to Baxter Springs himself and put you on a stage-coach. I swore to him that I'd leave you be until I delivered you safely home."

Warmth swirled through her. "Why didn't you tell me? I thought you were still upset with me!"

"His orders were no talking whatsoever. I was perched precariously on his bad side. I didn't want to risk tumbling off and cause you to lose your opportunity to earn that hundred dollars. The past six weeks have been the hardest of my life, Sam, not being able to let you know how I feel."

Her breath caught. "How is that, Matt?"

"I marched off to war when I was fourteen . . . and I stopped letting myself care about anyone . . . until you."

The fiddle started to send a lonesome melody around the room.

"'Nobody's Darlin','" Samantha whispered.

"You're somebody's darlin'. Dance with me, Samantha," Matt said as he wrapped his hand around hers.

His hand felt familiar in hers as he led her onto the

dance area, and she was reminded of the night they'd gone to scout out the river.

He took her in his arms and began to waltz. He held her so closely that his thighs brushed against hers.

She held his blue-eyed gaze as they moved in rhythm with the strains of the music. What an incredible journey they'd taken together. All because of a notice tacked on the wall of the general store and her determination to earn the money it offered.

"Are you going to continue to herd cattle?" she asked, hoping he might and that he might also come this way again.

He grinned. "Reckon I will, since it was my father's herd we were driving to market."

She widened her eyes. "That was your herd?"

"My father's. I was nothing more than a hired hand this trip. I was supposed to learn from Jake. Maybe I'll take my own herd up next year. We've got plenty of cattle left back at the ranch."

"That's the reason you felt such a responsibility toward me. Why you tried to protect me—"

"Maybe in the beginning, but over time, as I came to know you . . ." His voice trailed off, and an emotion both warm and inviting touched his eyes. "Take a walk with me."

Holding her hand, he led her out of the schoolhouse into the night. Light spilled from the windows, guiding their way until they stood beneath the spreading boughs of an ancient tree.

Limned by moonlight, he bracketed her face between his hands. "The truth is, Samantha, I was scared."

"Scared? Of what?"

"When I thought you were a boy, I was afraid I'd let you down like I had so many others during the war. I followed orders, Sam. Always. Even when I didn't agree with them. When the commanding officers ordered me to lead my unit into battle, I did. When I was ordered to advance, I did. Even when I thought retreat would have been better. A lot of boys died. I didn't want you to die.

"And when I found out you were a girl . . . when Jake ordered me to take you to Baxter Springs . . . I couldn't do it because I knew it was wrong—like so many of those orders I followed during the war. It felt good to disobey an order and to know I was right in doing it."

"I'm so glad you did, Matt. You should have seen my ma's face when I gave her that money."

"I didn't have to see her face, Sam. I saw yours . . . when we arrived in Sedalia and Jake handed you a hundred dollars. The look on your face made every mile worth it."

Reaching up, she touched his beloved face. "I'm sorry for the trouble I caused you, Matt, for having to lie."

"Don't be sorry, Sam. You not only turned out to be a good cowboy, but the girl I came to love."

He lowered his mouth to hers and kissed her tenderly. Six weeks of passion tethered and slowly released. As though they had all night. Or perhaps the rest of their lives.

And Samantha realized that more than a cattle trail, she'd followed her heart's trail.

DEAR READER:

I hope you enjoyed SAMANTHA AND THE COWBOY. My favorite part is when Matt discovers Sam's a girl—and realizes that he had stripped down to go swimming in front of her!

We're pleased to bring you more stories just like this one: BELLE AND THE BEAU is about an escaped slave who finds freedom and true love in 1859 Michigan, while ANNA AND THE DUKE is about a very proper English miss whose poetic soul longs for true love—and finds it. If you like bad boys, look no further than GWYNETH AND THE THIEF, a medieval tale.

There's an excerpt from each one on the next few pages—enjoy!

Abby McAden
Editor, Avon True Romance

FROM
BELLE AND THE BEAU
by Beverly Jenkins

"Are you warm enough?" Daniel asked Belle.

Wrapped in the heavy cloak, she nodded shyly. Her sixteen-year-old heart warmed at his concern. "Have your parents been helping runaways a long time?"

"Since before Jojo and I were born. Mama freed herself by running away from Virginia when she was twelve."

"Your mother was a runaway?"

"Yes."

Belle found that information surprising. It had never occurred to her that Mrs. Best was slavery born, but the knowledge gave Belle hope that one day she too could become as polished and confident as Mrs. Best. Right now, she didn't feel polished at all, but she was a free young woman.

In the silence that followed, Daniel said, "Well."

Belle felt shyer and more unsure than ever. "Well."

"Guess we should get going."

Belle nodded.

He then asked, "You sure you're warm enough? I know

it's warmer where you're from."

Belle nodded, again too overcome by being alone with him to form words. *He probably thinks you're a simpleton*, she scolded herself. "How far is the station?"

"Another few miles."

Back home, because there'd been no call for Belle to travel, or to be anywhere but sewing for Mrs. Grayson, she'd never seen a train except in pictures. "I've never seen a train station," she said without thought, then immediately wanted to take the words back.

A simpleton and *ignorant!*

Daniel sensed her discomfort, so he said gently, "That's nothing to be ashamed of. Lots of things will be new here. Think of yourself as a traveler in a strange land, and whenever you need help or have a question, remember we're all here."

Belle hadn't thought about being up North in those terms, but realized Daniel was correct; she was a traveler in a strange land.

"So will you let me know if you need anything?"

Belle looked him straight in the face. "I will."

"Promise?"

Holding his eyes, she said, "I promise."

"Good, now let's take you to see the station."

Belle wondered if she'd ever breathe again.

❧

FROM
ANNA AND THE DUKE
by Kathryn Smith

Gazing toward the bookshop shelves, Anna discovered the empty spot where Mr. MacLaughlin had found the book. His was the last copy. Swallowing her disappointment, she smiled at him. "I heartily recommend you buy the book."

His gaze never left her face, bringing a blush to her cheeks. "It wouldn't happen to be the book you came here to buy, would it?"

"It was," she replied honestly. "But I already have some of Byron's work at home. I'd hate to deny you the pleasure of discovering his poetry."

He offered the book to her. "I couldn't enjoy it knowing I took it from you."

How sincere he sounded! Anna's blush deepened. "Please. I insist." She couldn't explain it, not even to herself, but it was suddenly very important to her that he take that book.

He held the book to his chest with one large hand. "I've always been told it's rude to argue with a lady, so I won't. Thank you for your sacrifice, Miss Welsley."

Anna smiled. Was it warm in the bookshop or was it just her? "I'd hardly call it a sacrifice, Mr. MacLaughlin, but you're welcome. I hope you enjoy it."

"I shall think of you whenever I read it."

Anna's mother chose that exact moment to enter the shop. Anna could hear the sharpness of her voice from all the way at the back.

"I have to leave," she responded lamely, scarcely hiding her disappointment. "My mother is looking for me. It was a pleasure to meet you, Mr. MacLaughlin."

He didn't look as though he believed her, but he nodded. "The pleasure was mine." Even though they were strictly courtesy, his soft words sent a tingle down Anna's spine.

"And thank you again for allowing me the book."

She smiled, delaying leaving even though she could hear her mother's heavy footsteps coming closer. "Enjoy it."

"Anna," her mother's voice boomed from behind the next stack of books.

Anna started toward it, not wanting her mother to see this perfect young man. She wanted to keep him just for herself. Casting one last glance his way, she committed his image to memory so she would never forget the five incredible minutes she spent in his company.

"Good-bye, Mr. MacLaughlin."

He tipped his hat at her. "London's not that large, Miss Welsley, so I won't say good-bye just yet."

FROM
GWYNETH AND THE THIEF

by Margaret Moore

"I thank you for your generous hospitality, my lady," Gavin said in a low tone that seemed to make something inside her quiver, "but I really must be on my way. I have urgent business to attend to for my master."

Gwyneth planted her feet and crossed her arms, determined to act upon her plan. "You have to stay."

He frowned, his dark brows lowering. "*Have* to? Nay, I dare not. If I feel well enough to travel, I must, or my master will be angry."

"No, he won't. You have no master."

Gavin's frown deepened. "Why do you think that?"

"Because I saw you in the woods *before* you were hurt."

His expression grew stern as he grabbed her shoulders and pulled her close. His lips curled into a sardonic smile and his brown eyes seemed to flash with scorn. "A fine game you've been playing, with me the dupe. What will you do, lady? Turn me over to the king's justice? If you think to do that, you had better have more than ropes here."

She reached into her belt and pulled out her brother's

dagger which she had hidden there, putting the tip of the blade against his throat. "I have a use for you."

"Indeed?" he asked, one brow quirked in query as he eyed the dagger in her hands. "So that is why you put me here in this room and that fine bed. What is this use you have for me that requires you to house a thief in a fine chamber and give him such expensive clothes? You've treated me like a guest, except for the locked door. And the dagger at my throat, of course."

Before she could answer, a look of sudden comprehension dawned in his brown eyes.

"Somebody undressed me and combed my hair," he murmured as he circled her. "And I would have to be a fool not to know girls find me handsome. Since I am not a fool, I believe you do, too. Is that why you took pity on me, my young and pretty lady? Is that why you combed my hair and gave me your brother's clothes? What use have you for me here?"

She blushed hotly as she answered him. "You are an insolent rascal!"

"Sometimes." He smiled as he halted in front of her. "Don't you like rascals, my lady? Don't you find us . . . exciting?"